October Nights 3

Also by James B. Christensen

Honeymoon Phase

The Vessel

October Nights

The Sky Critters of Brockton County

October Nights 2

October Nights 3

James B. Christensen

ISBN: 978-0-578-81063-8 (Ravensbook)

For Tracey, Laura, and Abby

CONTENTS

Defenders of Earth

My name is Gracie, and I love spiders.

I didn't always. There was a time I feared them more than any other thing that lived. My worst "spider day" was the last day of summer when I was thirteen. It was hot out. I sat on the ground next to our house. I was trying to plant a daisy when this gigantic spider ran between my legs. It scared me to pieces. I screamed and jumped to my feet and tried to stomp it, but it got away and disappeared into the grass. What terrified me was how fast it moved.

I ran inside and told my dad about it and asked him to come find it and kill it. He laughed.

"We live in the country, hon," he said. "Spiders have a right to the outside."

We lived in a rural house in the middle of Nebraska. My dad's family used to own the land as far as you could see. They sold off parts of it, here and there. Eventually, it was my dad and me in the big old house with four acres around us. The rest of the land we used to own is corn-fields, but we don't grow it. Dad says the house and land will be mine someday. My mom is in heaven.

"No, they don't!" I said. "All spiders must die!"

"Why?"

"Because they're ugly!"

"Says who? Maybe your spider is Harry Styles to lady spiders."

"Huh? Yuck."

"And maybe spiders think you're ugly," Dad said.

He was busy putting folders and notebooks into his leather bag. He's a lawyer. Sometimes he has to go into town in the evening if someone gets arrested. He taught me to handle things at home by myself. I knew the emergency procedures. I knew the fire escape routes and safe rooms. I knew where the guns were and how to get them and use them if I had to. Dad told me the more I earned his trust, the more freedom he would give me. I worked hard for his trust and he gave me the freedom, like he said. I love my freedom. Out here in the country, you really feel free.

"Just think how big and scary you are," he said. "If I was a little spider and saw a giant like you jump up and screech, I'd run away, too."

"I didn't screech."

"I heard it."

"Well, I hate 'em. I'll kill it if I see it again."

"They eat the bugs, you know," he said. "Bugs are annoying. They bite and harass the hell out of us. I'll take spiders over bugs."

"Really?"

"What did the spider look like?"

"Huge. Mostly tan, with some black. Hairy."

"Sounds like a wolf spider."

"A *what?*" I said.

That was the creepiest thing I ever heard of. A *wolf spider???* That's like a "shark mosquito." Something that should not be. I was sure I'd have nightmares. The night was about to get far more interesting, though.

"Are they poisonous?" I asked.

"It'll sting if they chomp you. Won't kill you, though."

"Worse than hornet sting?"

"No."

That didn't sound so bad. I've had stings from bees and hornets and they *hurt*.

"They avoid humans, anyway," he said. "Especially loud, shrieking ones."

I gave him the eye roll.

"I guess they're okay," I said. "I hope I don't wreck his web by mistake."

"They don't make webs. They make burrows in the ground."

"Maybe I'll catch a few crickets. If I find his burrow, I can give him crickets."

"Now, that would be unfair to crickets. Just let the creepy-crawlies alone. They can work it out amongst themselves."

"All right."

"Why don't you give him a name? Then he won't seem as creepy."

That was a good idea. "I'll call him Herman, then."

"Herman, it is."

Dad's bag was packed.

"Alrighty, I'm off. Now, remember to shut off the oven after you cook your pizza."

"I know."

He gave me the Dad Speech. You've probably heard your dad give you one. It's funny. He knows I know that stuff. I know he knows I know, and so on. He says he has to say it even when he knows he doesn't have to, that someday I'll do the same. We'll see. Parents can be weird, but I'm thirteen and I've lived a little. I have to admit my dad might know more than I think. Still undecided on that.

I followed him outside and watched him get into his pickup. Caesar, our golden retriever, sat by my feet and also watched. I named Caesar after the ape from *Planet of the Apes*. I love those movies.

"Call if it's an emergency," he said. "No R-rated movies."

There he went again with the dad stuff.

"Caesar, you eat any bad guys, you hear?" he said.

Caesar ruffed at him. He was my bodyguard. He would eat anyone that threatened me. He proved it later that night.

Dad paused at the open door of the pickup and stared at me with a smile. He did that sometimes. It used to make me uncomfortable. By then I felt protected by it.

"Love you, Gracie," he said.

"Love you, too, Daddy."

"I'll be home after dinner. Want me to bring home some ice cream?"

"Yeah! But no nuts."

"I'll try to remember."

He winked and waved at me from the open window as he drove away. I watched until he drove down the long gravel driveway and turned toward town. We waved at each other again before he disappeared behind the trees. Then it was just me and Caesar.

I petted him for a while. He was a good boy, always calm and didn't get excited like most dogs. He made it easy for me to relax and pay attention to what was around me.

The sun was still a ways above the corn rows. Shadows were long and beautiful. The leaves had changed color. Half had fallen to the grass, which was in that in-between phase where it's thick and green but not growing as fast. This is Nebraska. At this time of year, it's hot in the day and cold at night. Now the breeze was chilly.

I went inside and put on my BTS hoodie and flip-flops. I hate shoes. Must be a country girl thing. I wanted to find the spider's burrow. Seemed impossible. Dad made me feel better about Herman, but I felt I would sleep better if I knew where he was.

It was hard to see through the thick grass and shadows. Caesar walked along beside me, nosing at the ground.

"I'm looking for a spider burrow, Caesar."

He watched me for a second, as if trying to figure out what that meant. I walked around the side of the house where Herman had surprised me. I stepped carefully, not wanting to destroy his burrow. Didn't want to be rude and make him mad. There was no sign of a spider burrow, and I realized I wouldn't know one if I saw it.

"Oh well, Caesar. There's no way I'll find it. He's outside, which is where I want him. Let's go in and have dinner."

Together we walked around to the front of the house. A shadow passed across the sun. A big one. Caesar noticed it and stood alert.

"Wow! What was that?"

We looked but didn't see what caused it.

"Probably a bird," I said. "A shadow that big must have been a bald eagle, maybe!"

The possibility of seeing a bald eagle kept me outside for another fifteen minutes. We watched the sky and treetops. No eagle, though.

It was dark by the time I cooked the pizza. I locked the doors and windows as Dad wanted. I watched a Disney movie. I still like them. Scary movies are cool, but not when I'm alone. Caesar ate the special dog food I gave him. We sat together on the couch and finished the movie after dinner.

I checked the clock when it was over. Dad would be home in an hour if his schedule held up.

I took my empty plate back into the kitchen. That's when things got weird.

Herman was on the counter. Hard to miss him against that white surface. I "screeched," dropped my plate, and it shattered. Caesar barked. Herman, though, didn't move. He just stood there. I thought he might be dead at first. I picked up the pieces of the broken plate and threw them away. Caesar watched Herman. It was funny. Caesar had his paws on the counter and his snout aimed right at Herman, who kept still. Dog and spider in a staredown.

After I took care of the mess, I joined Caesar at the counter to watch Herman. He still looked scary, but there was something about him that wasn't as intimidating as before. Even though he was still, I had this strange feeling he wanted something.

"What is it, Herman?" I asked.

Caesar ruffed, a little confused who I was talking to.

Herman just stood there. I wasn't sure what to do. For a few seconds we stood watching each other. Then I remembered what Dad told me to do with a spider instead of killing it. I took a paper plate out of the

13

cupboard, along with a drinking glass.

"Now, don't move, Herman. I want you to crawl onto the paper plate. I'm going to put you under the glass and take you outside. Keep still or I might crush you on accident."

He remained still as I came forward. I noticed the window was open a crack over the sink. Oops. That must've been how Herman got in. Dad wouldn't be happy if he knew I left a window open while he was gone. I made a mental note to make sure and shut it after I took care of Herman.

Before I looked away from the window, another spider came over the window sill from outside. Then another. And another. I was afraid again. I needed to slam that window shut, but now there a dozen spiders between me and the window!

Caesar didn't seem that interested.

"Hey, boy," I said to him. "What do we do here?"

Caesar watched me with a blank look. The decision, I guess, was mine.

Seeing no other option but to kill the spiders before more invaded, I hunched down so I could reach under the sink for a can of bug spray. There were drawings of spiders on the label, so I knew it would work. I was scared silly and my hands shook. I thought I might pass out, but I worried they would cover me in a giant web. Then I was even more scared. I reached out and steadied myself with Caesar's back. He looked at me, curious. Good ol' Caesar. Always being cool.

When I stood up, the spiders—led by Herman—had curled around and marched back out of the window. Caesar swung his head toward the back corner of the house and growled. All living creatures around me had lost their mind. I still thought about calling Dad. But he was talking to a client, and I didn't have much to tell him. Besides, he had taught me to take care of things, and that's what he needed me to do. It was dark out, but I had Caesar and a shotgun and that was enough to make me feel safe to go outside to see what was up.

"Come on, boy."

I loaded both shotgun barrels, then Caesar and I went out the back door. When we came down the front steps, he stood still like a statue with his nose pointed toward the back acre of our property. That was the woodsiest part of our land. Of course it was the woods. Whatever it was couldn't be in the flat areas lit up by the moon. Oh no.

I looked back at the outside wall under the kitchen window. Sure enough, there was Herman leading his pack (or whatever they're called) of spiders down the wall. They angled toward me and Caesar. I took it as a sign the critters wanted me to check the woods. So be it. I had the shotgun and had lots of practice with it. I held it ready and walked into the trees.

You should know that I wouldn't take any unnecessary risks. Dad wouldn't want that, and I'm no superhero. But this is life in the country. When you're far from help, you need to be ready to handle your business. A shotgun and a big dog can do that.

We were a third of the way into the woods when I saw the glow. It was green, like those glowing necklaces they give you at parties. I held the rifle steady.

"Anyone there? Just so you know, I have a shotgun. Don't jump out at me!"

I continued on. Caesar grew more agitated as we got closer to the green glow. I didn't know where Herman and his gang were, but I knew they followed us.

We came upon the source of the glow beyond an old, thick maple tree.

In the grass and leaves was a spaceship. Best I can describe it, its shape was like two bowls—bottom to bottom—with a bunch of plates between, but all very science-fiction with cool silver metal and glowing green lights. Other multi-colored blinking lights lined the middle. A green glow came from the bottom of the craft. Three little metal legs held it up.

Oh, and the whole thing was the size of a basketball.

Caesar barked at the object and almost scared me into firing the shotgun. I told him to calm down.

For a minute, I didn't know what to do. I remembered the shadow that had passed over in the late afternoon. By its trajectory, it made sense for the object to have caused the shadow and landed here. If I was right, the UFO had been here for a couple of hours.

Caesar got rowdy again and barked at the little craft. I was about to get after him again, when I saw what got him excited.

The glow was caused not by the ship itself, but by hundreds of tiny bug-like aliens that marched out of it. They moved so uniformly that it looked like glowing green ooze spreading out of the ship.

I dropped to my knees to take a closer look. The things had the size and appearance of a praying mantis, only they walked upright and had dark brown horns. All of this I could see by the glow of their bodies.

Seeing an alien space ship was not something I'd thought about a lot. When I did, I didn't picture this! I figured it would be like *Independence Day,* with tall aliens in gigantic ships. Now here it was for real, but with a little toy ship and bugs for aliens.

Caesar watched them pour out of their craft. He looked at me with a quizzical look, as if expecting me to know what to do.

"Beats me," I said. "Should we call the Air Force or something?"

He ruffed as if he had the answer. I stood up to think it over. It was a cool moment. Aliens have landed! Who would ever believe it?

Nobody, that's who. Not without proof.

Thinking of that brought me to my first decision—I must take a video of this. I needed my smartphone to do it. It was past my phone curfew. I figured Dad would understand.

As I turned to run back to the house, a strange and scary voice tore into my mind. It was the aliens. The language was one I'd never heard. A human voice box couldn't make those sounds. They spoke to me via telepathy. Caesar barked and leaped into the air. They were "mind-shouting" at him, too. I faced them again, and they stood still, looking at me.

They kept talking to my mind. Their language was gibberish to me.

16

They tried to tell me something.

"I can't understand you!" I said.

There must have been hundreds of voices talking at once. It was annoying and driving me crazy.

In my mind, I sent out a thought as loud as I could think it. *SHUU-UUUT UUUUUUP!*

It worked. The voices went silent. After that it was a stand-off. Me and Caesar stood and watched the aliens. Everyone waited for the other to do something.

"Who is your leader?" I asked out loud.

I didn't know if they had ears or not, but if I said the words out loud, I thought them, too, so I figured I had it covered.

The rows and rows of aliens parted as a larger, darker green alien came out of the bottom of the ship. He walked to the middle of his fellow aliens and stopped. I heard the mind-talking again, but it was only one voice this time. His voice. The gibberish had distinct sounds, and I realize now he (let's call it a "he") was trying different languages that he knew in case I could speak one of them. Of course I couldn't.

"I don't understand what you're saying," I said.

There was no answer. I shrugged, thinking maybe body language was an intergalactic thing. No response. I went into a long spiel about what my name was and where we were and this was Earth and this is my dog, Caesar, and so on. After a minute, I could tell we both understood there was a huge communication barrier.

The leader looked to his left and right. A message passed between their alien minds (I couldn't hear it this time) and the little green bugs moved out again. More aliens poured out of the spaceship. Caesar got restless.

Their commander stood still and stared at me with those beady black eyes.

"I'm going to call you Jules," I said. "I like to name things. Now, what are you doing here?"

Jules couldn't understand my words. But if he was smart enough to be in charge, he'd guess he had to tell me his intentions. As I thought about that, a weird dizziness took over my brain. I worried I would fall just as these swarms of space bugs were spreading over the ground.

An image came out of the fog in my mind. There was a sky in pastel colors. The image came with knowledge. I knew this imagery was from another planet. Their planet. I saw strange buildings standing at impossible angles. Everywhere were these little green bugmen. They flew in ships and walked around, going on with their lives. Then I saw war. The bug men set out in their ships to other parts of the planet. They conquered other aliens on their planet—aliens that looked like them, but different. I think the message was clear—we are conquerors. Now that we've conquered our planet, we're looking for another one. You're it.

I blinked out the vision to find the green glow all over the place.

"Do you have any idea how big Earth is?" I asked.

They must have an idea if they flew here. Pretty cocky to think they could take over Earth with their size and little ship. Or were there more coming?

I closed my eyes and thought of redwood trees, the Rocky Mountains, grizzly bears, the Marines, aircraft carriers, and Captain Kirk kicking alien butt for good measure. Jules hesitated, but his bugmen continued to fan out.

A thought came to me then—one of my own thoughts, I mean—and I giggled at the absurdity.

This was an alien invasion. Not a journey of exploring, but they were here to put me and the rest of humanity under their little green thumbs.

Jules came at my mind again. He returned my images of the military and nature and added his own bugmen crawling over everything. Maybe it was a silly thought, but what if they just kept coming? Millions and billions and trillions. How many would come before sheer numbers were too much for anyone to resist? Fine. I decided he was playing rough. Tonight I had learned that there were no limits to what was possible. Jules was serious. If I was Earth's first line of defense, I had to be serious, too.

I aimed the shotgun at his ship. Unless it was made of super-strong alien metal, a shotgun blast should smash it to smithereens. I watched Jules to see if he got the hint. Jules didn't seem threatened by the gun.

"You're new here," I said.

I almost fired, but I still couldn't. If I destroyed their ship, they couldn't leave. Then what? And how seriously should I take an attempted "invasion" by these little things? What if was a misunderstanding? What if they had the cure for cancer and stuff? Having aliens land was a big deal. Historic. I pictured newspaper headlines talking about how I massacred beings from another world. I'm not interested in making history, but if I did, that sure wasn't how I would want to do it. What would Dad say? I needed to know.

"I'm going to call my dad," I said to Jules. "He'll know what to do. Come on, Caesar."

Jules took his invasion up a notch. A pair of tiny red beams came out from his horns and hit me in the ankle. It stung like a hornet and I screamed. Caesar barked that nasty bark when he's ready to attack something. Then the beams hit Caesar, and he yelped.

That was enough for me. I shot at their ship. No super-secret space metal here. It blew apart like a coffee can.

Now the aliens let loose with their little lasers at me and Caesar. He chomped a few of them and spat them out. They must have tasted horrible. He shook his head like he ate black licorice. I couldn't help but laugh. I shot my second shell and blew away a patch of bugmen. I felt bad, but they started the intergalactic war, not me.

Hundreds of beams shot into me. I screamed at how badly it hurt. The shotgun was empty. Time to run.

"Caesar, come!"

He was under attack, too, and needed no coaxing to get out of there. We outran the bugmen. In seconds, we were out of range of their horn beams. What a weird night.

We stopped at the edge of the woods to catch our breath.

"Let's go call Dad," I said.

How to describe it? No clue. Telling him outright what had happened wouldn't work with most parents, but Dad would know I wasn't joking.

Caesar barked, and I came back to attention. The bugmen had surrounded us. Boy, they moved fast. Like Herman. My gun was useless unless I wanted to smash a few. But my body ached from the red beams. It felt like hundreds of hornet stings. The pain made me sick to my stomach. If they let loose again, I might pass out—maybe die. And I couldn't stand to think about them killing Caesar.

I didn't know what time it was. I guessed Dad was still a half-hour away from coming home when he said he would. Maybe he would come home early. What would he find? The bugmen might wait and ambush him. All I could think to do was buy time until I found a solution.

"Okay, I surrender."

Slowly, I placed the rifle on the ground. By now, Jules had come to the front of the pack. He looked at the shotgun and appeared to grasp my intentions. I waited for another round of beam stings, but they didn't come. Instead, I felt something tickling my feet.

Bugmen swarmed over my feet and up my body. Caesar growled at them, but stood his ground.

"Easy, boy. Let's see what happens."

I had a bad, bad feeling. They were up my legs to the knees. As they came up, they left glowing green stuff on my feet and legs. I realized too late that it was binding me, like being put in a cocoon.

"Oh, no!" I said. "Oh, no! Caesar attack!"

We'd never trained him to attack, but he knew what I meant. He was fearless. He tore into those dinky monsters and chomped 'em like a bowl of Purina. They shot their lasers at him. He tried to jump away and yelped from the pain, but he kept up the attack and killed them by the dozens. That was my good boy, Caesar.

They started shooting at me, too, and it hurt bad, but also made me mad. I struggled against the green webby gunk and it tore free. If they'd gotten me wrapped up, I would've been stuck. The webbing was up to my thighs. Another swarm of bugmen came at me to reinforce the webbing. Thousands of red beams hit me everywhere. I thrashed around, trying to escape. I screamed and flailed my arms. I thought I would go insane.

This was it, I figured. There was no getting away. There were too many of them and they moved too fast. The thought of them taking over earth wasn't such a laughable idea anymore.

I gritted my teeth and broke free of the webbing. The pain from the endless red beams made me weak, but if this was the end of my life, it was going to be a fight. I swatted the bugmen off my body.

"Get 'em, Caesar!"

He kept up his attacks. I stomped around on the creatures.

Then things got stranger. A cat came running into the mess and hissed at the bugmen. There were seven cats that came for milk and whatever I could give them. Soon all seven had arrived. Cats being cats, they spent too much time sniffing the aliens and playing with them and batting them around. I told them to stop playing and kill them. Cats being cats, they didn't listen, but their killer instinct took over soon enough.

A loud flapping blew my hair. A big owl swooped down and grabbed several bugmen and carried them off. Other birds came down. I felt hope. These animals sensed the threat and came running to fight for their home. I wondered if this was the instinct that made the animals walk onto Noah's ark.

There were still too many of the green bugmen. Not only that, their red beams took their toll on the birds and cats, and the animals had trouble dealing with the shock and pain.

Over the chaos, I heard a rustling through the leaves and grass. By the light of the moon, I saw the grass ripple as if someone had shaken a carpet. Out of the grass and onto the dirt near the tree line came Herman leading thousands of spiders.

"Oh, jeez. I hope Herman is on our side," I said.

The bugmen froze at the approach of Herman's army. Every terrible possibility went through my head. Herman was a descendant of the little things and had come to help them kill humanity. Thoughts like that.

However, Herman and his buddies didn't slow down. They plowed right into the bugmen. For the first time, the invading aliens were scared. Our counterattack had put a good dent in their numbers, so there weren't as many as before, but there were still plenty. Herman attacked a bugman. It was so vicious, I had to look away.

"Wolf spiders, bitches!" I yelled.

I'm glad Dad wasn't around to hear that.

There were so many spiders, and they attacked so fast and so hard, that me and Caesar and the other animals just stopped what we were doing and watched. The spiders came in waves. I thanked God they fought for us.

I'm not sure how I could keep track of Herman in the middle of it all. There were other kinds of spiders, too. Big and little ones, but Herman was the leader. He barreled right at Jules, the leader of the bugmen. Jules fired his red beams at Herman. While it rocked Herman back a little, Herman kept coming at him. The beams didn't affect the spiders as much, from what I could see.

Herman attacked Jules, and well, it wasn't pretty.

With their leader gone, the other bugmen scattered and panicked. It was as if the center of the hive mind went away and left them without direction. The bugmen regrouped enough to retreat into the forest. Herman led the spider army after them. Ha. That is funny to write—spider army—but that's what it was. The cats and birds gave chase, too. Just like that, Caesar and I were alone.

"That was weird," I said.

He looked at me with the most condescending expression I'd ever seen from him.

No kidding, it was weird.

We went inside, exhausted. I took two aspirin and gave Caesar a doggie painkiller. He had earned a treat, so I gave him a leftover hamburger from the fridge. I was sweaty and dirty, so I took a shower. It was then I saw my body covered head-to-toe with little red marks from where beams hit me. I hurt all over again seeing them. It looked the same as when I had chicken pox in the third grade. I planned to tell Dad the truth about what happened. I had no choice. There was no hiding the hundreds of red dots on my arms and legs and face. He would see them and demand to know what had happened.

He came home twenty minutes after I finished my shower. Caesar and I came outside to meet him. We sneaked a peek toward the woods. All was quiet. I knew Herman and his gang had finished the job.

Dad got out of his pickup with his briefcase and bag of ice cream from the store. He was tired, I could tell.

"How's my princess?" he asked. "Did you hold down the fort?"

"You could say that."

"Oh? Everything go okay?"

"Oh yeah."

I'd tell him the whole story later.

"Did you hear about the meteor?" he asked.

"What meteor?"

"Some meteor passing by," he said. "Astronomers were pretty excited about it. They tried to get a space probe to it so they could examine it."

"Really?"

"The space probe went quiet. That was a few billion down the drain."

He gave me a hug as he went into the house. It was too dark for him to see my welts. I wore long pajamas and slippers. I figured I'd wait until tomorrow to give him the story. He needed to rest, so I didn't bother him with it that night.

We had our ice cream and watched TV. He fell asleep during the news. Caesar and I went outside. I looked up and scanned the night sky. The stars are bright and beautiful out where we live. You can see shooting stars and satellites passing by.

It didn't take me long to find the meteor. If you look at the stars long enough, you can tell right away when something's out of place. It had a greenish tint to it. Caesar looked up at the sky and saw it, too. Were there other little lights coming out of the meteor? Maybe. Too far away and too hard to tell. Was that Jules's home planet or did he hitch a ride? Maybe it was a coincidence, and the green meteor was just a green meteor. I knew better.

Caesar ruffed, looking at the ground. There, in front of us, was Herman. I was excited to see him.

"Hey, Herman!" I said. "I'm glad you're okay. Thanks for taking care of things."

He stood there for a moment, then turned and crawled away.

"Good ol' Herman," I said. "I'll never kill a spider again!"

We walked up to the front porch and curled up in the porch swing. Caesar sprawled out across my lap, the big lug. I drifted off to sleep watching the stars over the trees that swayed in the breeze.

Sometime in the night, Dad came out and carried me to bed.

James B. Christensen

Bailey's New Shirt

Honor among the wicked might have prevented what happened. Small gestures amounting to a trifle to those with money and resources would have allowed certain things to continue on as they had for generations.

But there were no gestures, big or small. No honor. For that reason, Hazel Talley died alone and in miserable poverty in the oppressive cold of mid-December. For two weeks, her body went undiscovered until a man from the gas company, there for a meter check, noticed a horrible smell coming from the ramshackle house.

It was item one in the local news for a few days. For not only did the horrid circumstances of her death arouse short-lived pity, Hazel Talley was the mother of Arthur John Talley, a serial killer known as The Lumberjack for his preferred weapon. Talley played no favorites. He preyed upon young and old, male and female. He was caught and executed by lethal injection four years before. Hazel escaped blame. They considered her a decent soul who never deserved the hard life she lived and the bad men who inhabited her life, including her son, the bad seed.

Christmas festivities caught the public's attention, and the city of Monroe tried to forget Hazel Talley.

Otherworldly memories, on the other hand, are eternal. Eternal oaths, sealed in blood, are remembered always by minds not of the known world. As if expressing hellish rage over the death of Mrs. Talley, the winter of that Christmas season was brutal, windy, and stormy. Worse than anyone remembered.

The unpleasant reminder of the Talley case, along with the awful weather, cast a pall over the usual Christmas joy. In the Newey household, however, there was love and celebrating.

The family had little. Roger Newey just kept his clan fed and clothed with a hauling business in the warm months and snow removal in winter. He and his wife, Nita, raised their four children to view Christmas as a holy day and to temper expectations for piles of gifts. This was difficult to do when they saw the presents their friends received. But they were good kids, aware of their circumstances, and grateful for loving parents. Roger and Nita worked hard throughout fall and winter for a little extra shopping money.

Through their efforts, Christmas morning brought good news and bad news for Bailey Newey. The good news was a brand-new shirt. His wardrobe was sparse, so a new shirt was a welcome addition. It would give his appearance a little variety when school began in the new year. He liked the shirt. It was made from cozy flannel with a blue checkered pattern accented with purple. It felt nice, looked nice, and would keep him warm for the rest of the Midwestern winter.

The bad news? Also the new shirt. Bailey more or less wore the same pair of jeans every day, topped with one of four T-shirts and button-up shirts. A different garment in the mix would at once get the attention of school bullies who were on the lookout for such things. Wearing the new shirt on the very first day back from Christmas break was an invitation to a full day of being mocked, laughed at, or worse. Such an item had to be worked in gradually, not right away.

There was no choice but to wear the shirt on the first day back, though. His family had next to no money. That he and his two younger siblings got any gifts at all was a testament to the extra hard work his parents had put in to have a few more dollars for the holidays. His mother would watch to see if he wore the new shirt, just as his tormentors would watch. To not wear the shirt was to reject the gift, to show shame and lack of gratitude. That he could not do. He would absorb his punishment for the sake of his mother's feelings.

So on a January morning, for the first day back to school after the holiday break, Bailey put on the shirt and buttoned it up as he fought the nagging, twisting knot in his stomach. He came out for breakfast. His mother complimented him on how nice he looked. He smiled sheepishly and did an effective job of hiding his anxiety.

He stared out the school bus window as it rumbled along slick roads. Bailey had his driver's license, but the Newey family had only Roger's truck. So Bailey biked in the nice weather and took the bus in the winter. He was the only student of driving age who still took the bus and never heard the end of it.

It was still early. Gray winter clouds hid the rising sun. Snow covered everything. It formed a muddy slush in the road. There was no color, no brightness. Bailey hated winter as much as he hated school, but he tried his best to follow his father's example and count his blessings and be strong. He reminded himself that his path on earth was only a small part of his journey, that a better, more rewarded life waited on the other side of eternity.

The bus started up the road to the schoolhouse. Bailey never liked the building. They put it up in the 1930s. A landslide from the surrounding hills had buried the original school. It had happened on a weekend, so there were few deaths. The school was mostly undamaged, but it was under so much rock and dirt that the decision was made to build a new school on top of the old one. They sealed the old school. It was forbidden for anyone to enter, but adventurous types always found a way in to explore the abandoned, subterranean classrooms.

The new building looked to Bailey like a cathedral to an unholy religion. It had no symmetry and lots of jagged points and angles. It wore a coat of peeling dark gray paint. He felt as though the building was designed just to make him feel unwelcome. If so, it worked.

His classmates started in on him the moment he entered the classroom. Of course they noted the new shirt. Not to compliment it, but to mock it. How dare he? How dare he try to look a little nicer? How dare he try to take a little pride or show a little dignity? They even improvised a song about it. Deep down, Bailey had to admit it impressed him. Just when he thought their creative depravity couldn't reach any lower, they came up with a new way to get at him.

He kept his head down and took his seat at the head of his row. Naturally, his assigned seat was at the front of the class. It was foolish to hope a teacher would have enough sense to let a bullied student have a seat far away from the alpha males and females that made sport of the weaker kids.

To his left was Brittany. She was pretty. Not just rich-kid-in-fancy-clothes-and-hairdos pretty, but the real thing. She didn't bully him aggressively. Her tactic was to condescend to him, to invite him to fancy parties she knew he didn't have the clothing for, or to ask him about the latest gadgets and doodads she knew he couldn't afford.

She was seated when Bailey entered. He took his seat, and she took longer than necessary to give Bailey's new shirt the once-over. Her look was never one of disgust, but of fake pity, which was far worse.

"Nice shirt, Bailey. Did you get it at Roderick's?" she asked.

Brittany knew he couldn't afford even a pair of shoelaces at a fancy store like Roderick's. He looked away as he shook his head in answer to her question. He didn't need to see her look of malevolent satisfaction, because he'd seen it before.

On his other side was Teddy Wright. Teddy was the opposite of Brittany, not just in gender but in everything else. While Brittany would've been radiant even in sackcloths and ashes, Teddy was nothing but a creation of his parents' wealth. He wasn't handsome, intelligent, or sophisticated. He was athletic, but much too short to excel at anything. Like most of the little-fella bullies in school, Teddy maintained (and funded) friendships with large upperclassman who served as his muscle. Take away the money, fancy clothes, and intimidating friends, and Teddy was just another blustering loser.

Bailey knew from his upbringing that he was to pray for his enemies and to do good to those who hurt him. Teddy put that philosophy to the test like no one else. But as Bailey's father told him, if the philosophy didn't apply in circumstances created by people like Teddy, what good was it? So Bailey prayed for Teddy and hated him at the same time. He hoped God would understand.

So Bailey spent a few minutes before the class bell rang, hearing about how stupid and ridiculous his new shirt was. He knew this was coming, but he endured it anyway for the sake of his mother. He took pride and comfort in that, at least.

"Did your mommy get that shirt at the thrift store?" Teddy asked.

"No," Bailey said, infuriated by the question.

His parents had worked hard to earn extra money so they could have the pleasure of going into the retail store and buying the shirt for him, brand-new. Teddy, of course, knew which words to pick that cut the deepest.

Teddy laughed. "Oh yeah? If they bought it new, how come it has a thrift store tag in the bottom there?"

Numbing terror gripped Bailey's arms and legs. At first, he hoped it was just a case of "made you look," but he glanced down to where his shirt was tucked in. There he saw the small thrift store price tag attached at the side seam.

Bailey stared at it as the class erupted in derisive laughter. He cursed himself and his family. None of them had noticed it. Talk about opening the door into your own face. The next sixty seconds were the worst Bailey had ever endured in that hideous house of horrors called the school building. Finally, the teacher arrived only seconds before the final bell rang. He looked around, curious at the ruckus. Perish the thought he would be inquisitive enough to ask what happened.

Bailey was the first one out of the classroom when history let out. He moved fast enough to escape added torment, but slow enough to keep his dignity. Teddy and Britney didn't attack him directly. They mocked him to each other in conversation. He overheard everything, as they intended.

The pair lost interest in him. Bailey was then, finally, alone and unnoticed. He ducked into the men's room to catch his breath and collect his thoughts.

He paced back and forth in front of the row of sinks. His hands clenched and relaxed. He did not like the look of the young man staring back at him as his reflection passed from mirror to mirror. He didn't see hurt or fear, but a seething, dangerous rage. That alone was unsettling, but there was something more in the reflection. Power. Raw, intimidating power. It made Bailey's arms and legs shake.

In a fury, he yanked the shirt out of his pants and stared at the price tag. Never in his life had he hated an object so much is that unassuming square of paper. It had a purple dot on it, signifying that it had been on clearance. Even in the thrift store, all Bailey could hope for was the bottom of the barrel.

By now his anguish boiled so hard that an icy calm settled over his mind and spirit. He removed the price tag and dropped it in the trash. He glanced at the clock. Only a minute until the next class. Neither Britney nor Teddy were in his next class, but news of his shirt had certainly spread throughout the entire school by now. Even teachers were probably guffawing about it in their lounge. There was nothing to do but endure it. As usual. He hoped everyone would just get bored with him. Sometimes they did. Sometimes they didn't.

As he tucked the shirt back in, he noticed a small stain on the tip of the shirttail. He took a close look. It was a dark rust color, probably from the previous owner. Spilled tomato juice or something like that.

Bailey loved his mother very much, but in that moment he burned with rage at her. And to himself. Like a fool he had wandered into school on the first day back from Christmas break wearing a used, stained shirt. Bailey shook his head in disbelief.

You put the "kick me" sign on your own back.

That voice entered his mind so loudly he thought someone had entered the restroom unnoticed. He looked in the mirror again. The person looking back at him with that face so full of anger? He might have said it.

Unable to tamp down his anguish, Bailey punched the paper towel dispenser. The blow ripped it free from the wall. It crashed to the floor in pieces.

He caught his breath as his head cleared. It felt good to hit something, but now he feared a lacerated or broken writing hand. His hand was unharmed. The dispenser was smashed and useless. Paper towels spilled everywhere.

Bailey frowned at the scene. He glanced at the mirror, trying to see the situation from a fresh perspective. The eyes looking back it at him reflected a calm, steely anger. It was a look Bailey had never seen in the mirror.

Felt good, didn't it?

That voice in his head again. Bailey stood up straight. Something felt different. He strutted to the sink and watched himself.

They need to be dealt with.

Bailey frowned. The reflection frowned back, of course, but the darkness in the eyes remained. Bailey knew who needed to be "dealt with." But how? Why was his mind working like this? Lots of questions.

The first bell rang. Baily hustled out of the restroom before they discovered his vandalism.

Things were calm until lunchtime. Students gathered in the hallway to talk and fool around in the few minutes they had left before the afternoon class began. Bailey stood with the other poor kids and talked for a while. The poor kids had a love/hate relationship. They reminded each other of their low status, but each other was all they had.

That uncertain feeling of power and danger that had coursed through Bailey's body was gone. He felt a mixture of relief and disappointment.

Teddy came by the group. He made a few cutting remarks regarding their clothing, their lineage, and dared them to respond. Bailey felt his fingers and toes prickle as power surged again. He glared at the little

31

bully. Bailey's role was to look away and wait out the torment. But his fear had gone, replaced with an urge not to avoid confrontation, but to take it to unspeakable lengths. What he wanted was for Teddy to see the hatred in his eyes.

"What're you looking at?" Teddy asked.

Bailey stood up straight and stepped closer to Teddy so they stood facing each other.

"A sawed-off little ferret who forgot his bodyguards," Bailey said.

His voice was low. Everyone, Teddy included, looked at him in shock. The bully stepped back when confronted by a taller man. Infuriated by this reflexive show of weakness, Teddy recovered and looked ready to start a fistfight.

Bailey, trying to manage the dueling emotions, knew this wasn't the time nor place to settle things with Teddy. He stepped back.

"I'm sorry, Teddy. I didn't mean to look at you," Bailey said.

Teddy frowned at him, skeptical. He grinned, and the darkness in Bailey rose again.

"It won't happen again. I promise," Bailey said. "Shake on it?"

Teddy frowned. His simple mind did not understand how to process Bailey's erratic behavior. He looked at Bailey's outstretched hand. Another wry grin spread across Teddy's face. Bailey knew the little thug was already thinking how he could use a handshake to inflict pain.

Teddy took Bailey's hand and squeezed. Bailey squeezed too. To everyone's surprise, Teddy dropped to his knees in pain. The short bully had found himself in the grip of someone like Bailey's father, who had hands like grizzly paws.

This was new territory for everyone. The incident had attracted a large crowd. Teddy was lost in humiliation. He got to his feet and ran. The bell rang, summoning everyone to their next class. The crowd dispersed before any conversation about it could begin.

Bailey shuffled off to his next class. He made a mental note that after last bell he had to leave school quickly. There was no way to predict what the fallout would be from the sudden turnabout he had pulled on Teddy. One thing Bailey knew—Teddy was going to run to his large friends and let them take the revenge. Bailey might have to get his father involved for the sake of his own safety. He hated to do it. You never know how a parent is going to react, and sometimes it makes things worse instead of better in the long run. Bailey learned at a young age that it wasn't just kids who form themselves into groups to pick on and bully others. Grown-ups did it, too.

He rushed out of school. Taking the bus home seemed like a bad idea. His bullies would jump on with him and wait for their opportunity. He decided to take a meandering path home and try to evade Teddy and the others.

He was almost to the end of the block. Once he rounded the corner, he could disappear into the tree-lined streets of the neighborhood and make his way home. If he needed to, he knew the sidestreets to take to escape Teddy and his bodyguards. If he got a good enough head start, his plan might work.

Todd, one of Teddy's big friends, rushed out of the school. He was alone. Bailey assumed Teddy was with the other bodyguard, watching over the other exit.

Bailey took one more look back as he turned the corner and made eye contact with Todd. The big kid broke into a sprint, coming after Bailey like a dog chasing a rabbit. Bailey saw him and quickened his pace. He didn't want to lower himself to run unless there was no other choice.

Don't you dare run, you wimp.

Bailey slowed to a walk, obeying the new inner voice.

"He's too big," Bailey said out loud, to the voice. "I really screwed up. I've seen that guy bloody people up."

Stay and fight. You'll win. You'll win so good he'll bother no one again. Ever. I promise.

Bailey remembered punching the paper towel dispenser in the bathroom and his undamaged hand. He remembered the look from the reflection in the mirror that was his own face yet somehow not his face.

33

And that voice. Where did it come from? Something strange was happening. Bailey felt new realms of fright.

It should have been an easy decision to run, but it wasn't. Bailey fought against himself. There was a new part of himself demanding a place in his psyche, a longing for violence hard to resist. Was this what happened when bullied kids were pushed too far?

Todd was a block-and-a-half away. Bailey knew his pursuer wouldn't tire. He was on the football and track team and in shape. Bailey couldn't outrun him. His escape hinged on getting far enough ahead that Todd couldn't guess his path. That plan was already out the window. Outrunning Todd wasn't an option. Bailey was terrified.

He knew, from walking and biking these streets in the warm months, that an empty lot sat between two houses. That lot led into the woods. Bailey spent a lot of calm, lonely hours in those woods and knew them well. It was a shortcut to his house. Chances were good he could lose Todd in the thick trees. He cut through the lot and ran through the snow. He was already near exhaustion.

Todd saw Bailey's intentions and ran harder.

The big kid had almost closed the distance when Bailey ran into the trees. Panic filled Bailey's heart and mind. Something about Todd's face scared Bailey. He knew what was behind it. Wearing a new shirt and trying to improve his appearance was bad enough, but he had stood up to Teddy and humiliated him in front of others. Word had already spread. Bailey deserved punishment.

Bailey hoped his father would be home if he made it. Todd roared and cursed in a white-hot fury. He picked up a thick branch and slammed it into tree trunks as he passed. He promised murder and torture. Bailey believed him. He feared he wouldn't make it out of the woods alive.

He's going to kill you, and you know it.

Bailey wanted to argue with the voice, but it was right. He wasn't halfway through the woods, and still Todd drew closer. Bailey was losing energy. He could barely run through the deep snow anymore. His lungs burned. His thighs wobbled. Fighting Todd at full strength was impossible, and now Bailey was exhausted.

Surrender to me, and he won't bother you again.

Something's wrong, Bailey thought. I can't fight him.

Surrender to me, or you'll die.

Bailey gave in and stopped resisting the voice. What happened next Bailey saw through his eyes, but with a feeling of not being there.

He stopped and let Todd close the distance. The bigger kid raised the branch to swing at his head. Murder was in his eyes. Bailey knew Todd had gone over a dangerous edge. This wasn't to be any by-the-numbers butt-kicking. This was the big time.

Todd swung the branch. Bailey raised his arm to block. The wood smacked his elbow. He yelled out. Todd swung again and again, hitting Bailey's shoulder, legs, and ribs. Pain exploded throughout his body. Bailey pleaded with Todd to stop, but Bailey knew it would not stop. Not this time.

Surrender.

Bailey surrendered.

As Todd brought the branch down for another strike, Bailey drew back and punched the bully hard on the jaw. Bailey enjoyed the feeling. The punch drew power from his arms, back, and legs. Bailey never knew how hard a person could punch if they knew what they were doing.

Todd fell onto his back, sinking six inches into the snow. He was shocked, but recovered and staggered to his feet. Blood trickled from his mouth where his teeth had torn his cheek and lips.

Like a madman, Todd rushed again. Bailey dropped him with right and left punches. A hook to the liver dropped Todd back to the snow with a gasp. This time, Todd stayed down, uncertain and looking scared.

"Now you know how it feels," Bailey said.

It was his voice, but low and slow. Someone else chose the words.

"Get up and leave, and this is as far as it goes," Bailey said. "If you come at me again, we're going all the way. Understand?"

The shock of Bailey's counterattack faded. Todd got to his feet, determined. Backing down was something Todd had never done and didn't understand. Bailey tried to reassert control of his body, terrified of what was to come.

Todd rushed again. Bailey stood aside and tripped the brute. Todd fell face first into the snow. Bailey pounced on his back like a tiger. He fought his way a face-up position, but Bailey still had him pinned. Todd punched. Bailey deflected. He doled out several blows until Todd was dazed and subdued.

Bailey figured it was over, but found himself piling snow onto Todd's face. Todd tried to fight back, but was too addled and his strength had left. He kicked and thrashed as Bailey continued to bury his face.

"I WARNED YOU!" Bailey screamed.

Soon an icy mound of heavy, wet snow covered Todd's head. He tried to kick his way out. Bailey likewise buried his ankles and then his wrists. In minutes, Todd stopped moving.

Bailey stood and caught his breath. The surge of power still held his body. After another ten minutes, Bailey felt himself return to normal. He stared at Todd's body in shock. He dropped to his knees and pawed the snow away from Todd's head. It was too late. Todd was dead. Bailey was numb.

"I killed him!"

No, you didn't. It was self defense, anyway.

"I'll go to prison."

I'll take care of it. Surrender again.

Bailey lacked the will to resist, and the presence took him over again. He carried Todd's body to a snowy ravine and tossed him in. Despite the horror of the situation, Bailey felt a thrill from the surging strength running through his limbs.

"They'll look for him. They'll find the snow messed up and they'll find him."

As he spoke, thick flakes of snow fell. They landed on his shoulder and hair and also covered Todd's body.

Bailey smiled.

Big snow coming tonight. Won't be the last one of winter by a long shot. No one will find him 'til spring.

"But I'll have to live with it forever, either way," Bailey said.

He would have killed you. You know that.

The force left his mind and body. Bailey walked home.

He was quiet at dinner. He left the table after the meal and did his homework. His siblings tried to get him to play with them. He just sat and stared at the television. Concerned looks passed between his parents. Bailey noticed, but ignored it. Bailey threw on his coat and went outside. It was a frigid night. He barely noticed. He trudged through the snow and sat under the willow tree in their yard.

The sun was gone when his father came out to join him.

"I know something happened today," Roger said. "Do you want to talk about it?"

Bailey was silent for a moment. Luckily, his clothes hid the bruises and scrapes from his confrontation with Todd. His father waited.

"I popped a bully today," Bailey said.

Roger raised his eyebrows and smiled a little. Bailey didn't look at him. He just sat there, stewing.

"Did he start it?" Roger asked.

"He's been starting it for ten years."

"You know what I mean."

"Yeah, he started it."

"There was no other way out of it?"

"No."

"Was he going to hurt you?"

"He did. Hammered me with a big tree branch."

"But you took care of him?"

"I did. Was I right to do it?"

Roger sat next to Bailey. "If you had no choice, and it was in self defense? Yes.

Bailey felt a little better, but he couldn't reveal how far his self-defense had gone.

"Who was it?" Roger asked.

Bailey didn't answer.

Roger nodded. "I understand. Will I hear from the school?"

"Not unless he squeals. I don't think he will."

"You need me to speak to someone at the school?"

"Won't do any good. You talking to the school won't do any good. Me popping the bully won't do any good. I'm just gonna have to walk around with my head down. No matter how hard I fight, no matter how much you talk to the principal, it's gonna come around to the same thing. There's always another bully, and there's only one of me."

Roger sat next to him. They watched the moon light up the snowy horizon with a silver glow.

"No, it isn't gonna come around to the same thing," Roger said. "Not this time. I know we're poor, son. I wish things had been different, but I made a gamble that hard work would be enough. Turns out there were things I didn't know. But I can promise you this—if you need to handle some business and you can do it, then you handle your business. I will back you up. If it takes the rest of your schooling years to get the message through to these bullies and teachers and anyone else, then so be it. It will be worth it. You understand?"

Bailey looked at his father for the first time, searching his eyes to make sure he understood.

"Just make sure you're in the right. It's your only hope."

"Okay," Bailey said.

"And remember that I'm here for you. No matter what. So don't hold back on me. If you need help, say so."

Bailey was quiet.

"Is there anything you want to tell me?"

Bailey shook his head, anguished to keep his father in the dark, but it was too surreal to put into words. He worried about putting his father in danger.

Roger sensed there was something to come out, but there was no forcing it. He patted Bailey on the thigh and stood.

"Let's get inside," he said. "Your mother got some hot chocolate."

After the hot chocolate, Bailey watched television until it was bedtime. He had a corner of the basement to call his own. An old mirror hung on the wall. He stood before it and once again saw an expression that was angry yet somehow amused at its own anger.

Bailey felt a sudden urge to do something physical. He thought about challenging his hulking father to an arm wrestling contest, but figured that would arouse suspicion if he did well. For now, he wanted to keep his supernatural inner conflict to himself.

So he dropped to the concrete floor and started a series of push-ups. He did them fast and kept going. He normally could do twenty before he tired. That night, he made it to thirty without slowing. By the time he grunted and strained to push himself upright one last time, he had done seventy-five push-ups.

He stood and glared at the mirror, enjoying the look of savage glee that stared back at him. He dropped to his bed and stared at the bare bulb on the ceiling. What had come over him? He supposed it was possible this was a mental change manifesting physically. That seemed unlikely. He smiled. It was the smile he saw in the mirror. A new look.

"I'm in charge," he said.

It took a long time for Bailey to fall asleep. He stared at the ceiling and tried to make sense of the crazy day. It didn't seem real. Any of it. He told himself if he went back to the ravine, Todd's body wouldn't be there. There would be nothing but undisturbed snow. He knew better, but hoped if he repeated that version of reality in his mind, it would come true.

It wasn't guilt he felt so much as a sense of dissociation from reality. Todd had meant to kill him. He had no sense of consequence or boundaries. Bailey realized he'd lived with an odd sense of comfort in the familiar, even though it was unpleasant. Bailey was bullied once in a while, and the wheels rolled on. Now things were different, unknown. It was Bailey's hands that killed Todd and hid the body, but some other force drove the movements. Bailey had surrendered to it. Was he innocent? Bailey ached to speak to his father about it. For now, keeping things secret seemed the safest route for everyone.

"Who are you?" Bailey asked. "Who's in my mind?"

There was no answer. Did the invading force sleep? Bailey shifted onto his side.

"I'll call you Hyde," he said.

Giving the entity a name gave him an odd sense of peace and authority. He drifted into a dreamless sleep.

On Saturday, Bailey stirred awake earlier than usual. He knew it was Hyde that had rousted him from within. He put on the new shirt and was buttoning it up when the voice came.

Go to the library. I want to show you something.

He walked to the library in the winter cold. Inside, he found the aisle containing the crime books. Hyde guided his movements. For the moment, Hyde's force and Bailey's mind coexisted. He continued to think about all that had happened. While the shirt's power had given him increased strength and a more assertive attitude, he had not sought to kill anybody. He had used the power—or more accurately, it had used him—for self-defense. He had no urge to kill for sport—especially an innocent person. But how long would that last? What of those who were not so innocent? Hard to tell where the line was drawn.

At eye level, there were three books about a local killer who made headlines around the country four years ago. Bailey found it hard to breathe. The possibility crowding his thoughts just couldn't be. The killer was Arthur John Talley. The serial murderer who ravaged the city and was executed for it. His parents had discussed it in hushed tones over the dinner table. His parents had forbade Bailey and his siblings from being out and about on their own even during the daytime.

His hands shook as he took the books one at a time to an empty table in an isolated corner of the library. It didn't take long to get the broad strokes. Arthur John Talley, before they knew his name, was called

"The Lumberjack" in the press because of his choice of an ax to kill his victims. There were pictures of the victims in happier circumstances. Bailey felt ashamed of himself for being disappointed there were no crime scene photos.

His heart stopped when he saw a picture of Talley before they had caught him. The photo was from a family gathering. Everyone, including Talley, smiled and posed for the camera. It gave Bailey a chill to think everyone surrounding Talley was unaware of his ax hobby. But what got Bailey's attention was Talley's wardrobe.

Talley wore the same shirt in the photo that Bailey wore now. He was sure of it. The colors and pattern were the same. Hard to believe any possessions of Talley's could have escaped the police. Bailey wasn't sure how those things worked. Somehow, the shirt went unnoticed until donated to the thrift store. After a certain period of taking up space on the clothing rack, it had been marked down for a quicker sale. Now it was on Bailey's back.

Bailey stared out the window to the slush and snow as it came together. The stain on the shirt was not tomato juice or spaghetti sauce, but blood. Not only had the garment belonged to Talley, he had worn it during at least one of his murders. As Talley carried out his ghastly duties in the shirt, a dark power had transferred into the garment. And that power—increased strength, aggressiveness, and a lack of fear—had now passed to Bailey. One little drop was all it had taken. It was incredible and impossible to deny. But there was more.

He checked the pictures again. In most of them, the ones taken after Talley's arrest, showed a dark and glowering look—the same look that came over Bailey when he saw himself in the mirror.

Bailey sat back and thought about what he'd learned in the context of recent events. Talley's essence allowed him to defend himself. But Talley wasn't a warrior for the oppressed. He killed innocent people among other bad deeds. How long would Talley dwell within him? Would things progress to total possession? What was the end game? Was protection from bullies worth an eternal reckoning? Bailey knew his situation was what his father called a "handshake with the devil."

"I want out," Bailey said, quietly.

It's too late. Besides, you're powerful now. Most people never know that feeling.

You want something from me? Bailey asked. You want me to be a serial killer like you?

No. I need something else from you. But first, I have to show you something else.

I have to get home by lunch to help my father. He already suspects something.

You'll be home in time. Let me show you, and you'll understand.

I don't want understanding. I want to be free.

Help me and we'll both be free.

Talley guided Bailey first to the corner pharmacy to buy a small flashlight, then to the school. The building was quiet and empty for the weekend. Bailey followed the impulses given to him by Talley's essence. It was still a couple of hours until lunch time at the Newey home. Time was short, depending on what Talley had in mind.

The school building sat on the outskirts of the city. Because of the landslide and the resulting construction of the new school on top of the old, the building appeared to sit on a hill. Debris from the long-ago landslide surrounded it and had become the natural landscape. A tall flight of stairs led to the school's front door.

Bailey went around the side of the school. The ground had been leveled off for practice fields and basketball courts. Beyond these was a chain link fence with signs warning against going beyond the barrier. This was what schoolkids knew as the Forbidden Zone. It was where determined students and adults tunneled into the abandoned school house for parties and whatever else they did. The police kept a close eye on it. The city filled in tunnels as they found them.

Bailey climbed the fence and looked around. No one was watching. Because of Talley's essence, Bailey didn't have to search for an entrance. He went high into the hills, far past where any holes and tunnels had been found and blocked. He kept going until he found a thick old tree in a wooded area. At the base of its trunk was a pile of branches.

As if he'd done it hundreds of times, Bailey removed the branches and a hole appeared where he expected it. He crouched down and looked inside. Only dirt and darkness. He shined his flashlight into the opening. It ran out of sight.

It's okay. Go down.

He slid down the frozen dirt and into blackness. After a minute, his feet touched something solid. He turned on his flashlight to see what it was.

Steps.

He put his boots down and stood. The flashlight lit up a stone stairwell. The path was clear. He descended until he came to a wall. A door-sized opening was smashed away. He stepped through.

Bailey swept his flashlight around an empty, abandoned classroom. He was in the sealed off school that had been buried long ago. It was illegal to be here, he knew, but the hidden entrance and tunnel, along with the stairway and open wall, told him he wasn't the first.

The classroom door was secured from the inside with four deadbolt locks and an iron barricade. It took him a few minutes to get the door open.

He passed through the classroom and out into the hallway. It was like coming out of a time machine and into the 1950s. His grandfather went to this school, walked these halls. Ancient lockers in rows and old-fashioned linoleum floors. It was cool and eerie at the same time.

He didn't have to wander. He went down the main hall, downstairs to the old gymnasium, into the locker room, and through a forgotten closet. In the back of the closet was another door. It was hard to see if you weren't looking for it. One could just make out the seams on the wall. It was hidden. Again, he was nervous.

I'm telling you, you don't have to be afraid.

He searched for a way to open the door. There was no handle. He felt around the edges. Nothing. On the floor he found a length of rope. He took up the rope to move it out of the way. It was attached to something. He pulled. The door squealed open.

Another stairway waited for him. Again he explored with his flashlight. Stone steps wound down in a spiral. He took a deep breath and checked his watch. Still on schedule for lunch, but there was no time to waste. He descended the steps as fast as he could without stumbling.

He came out into a wide and high chamber carved from the earth. His flashlight gave off just enough light to show it all. A rectangular cube of stone sat in the center. It was painted red, but Bailey knew it wasn't paint. A hole in the ground, with a ten foot diameter, sat next to the stone block. A wooden bridge, flanked by five-foot high side rails, arched over the hole.

Bailey crept up to the hole.

I wouldn't get too close. It's still sleeping, but you never know what might wake it up.

"Wake what up?"

Look at the walls.

Bailey moved his flashlight over the walls, revealing crude murals—in the same red substance—depicting a large serpent-like creature. It was a giant, compared to the humanoid figures painted alongside it. The monster was pictured in space, in the sea, underground, eating humans.

"What is that? Looks like a moray eel."

It is of the same family. But a special one. Older than the mountains.

Is it like Nessie? Some kind of lake monster?

Not even I would dare put its name in your thoughts. Sit.

Bailey sat in front of the altar.

In life, I took people for the eel.

"You were some kind of hunter for that thing?"

A few I killed for fun, because I had a compulsion to do it. Others I brought to the eel. Some were killed because they learned too much or saw what they shouldn't have seen, or got chatty when they were drunk. I did this for those who feed the eel. They've fed her for centuries.

"They? It wasn't just you?"

I wasn't the first one they brought into the Cult of the Eel. I'll bet some of those bullies you deal with are also in the club, just as their parents are.

"Is that why I'm here? You want me to join?"

I want you to destroy them.

"How can I do that? They're powerful, from the sounds of it."

The eel is asleep for a season. The cult will not meet for a while. And there's nothing to fear. Surrender to me. I'll do the heavy lifting and set things right.

"Set things right? You were a serial killer. You did horrible things. Now you want me to believe you want to do the right thing?"

I made mistakes and got caught. We struck a deal for my silence. They reneged. If you help me, I will have my revenge, your tormentors will be gone, and my soul will go on.

"Go on? Where? To hell?"

By destroying the evil disciples of this demonic creature, I hope to restore my soul. The anguish of this existence is unbearable.

"If I say no?"

The cult will continue to prey on the innocent. And I will haunt you to your dying day, which I may bring to you sooner than you'd like.

"And if I—we—succeed?"

I'll leave you. You can go back to your life, free and without suspicion.

Bailey sat silent for a moment. "I guess I have no choice."

That was Saturday morning. By Sunday morning, after a night of violent winds and storms, six prominent citizens had disappeared. Business owners, members of high society, and government officials. All vanished in a single night.

Reporters and news crews from across the state converged on Monroe. It was a frenzy for a couple of days, but it soon evened out. By

Wednesday, national attention had faded, but local interest remained intense. Rumors spread, mutated, and became more bizarre by the telling. The City of Monroe was afraid again.

Bailey wore the shirt every day as he had since the confrontation with Todd. Yet Talley's essence faded. Bailey more or less returned to his normal self just in time to avoid a sit-down with his concerned father. Talley had yet to reveal the final plan, so Bailey went about his days with a gnawing ache in his gut.

Things at school were somber and muted. The bullies stood down. Todd's disappearance had struck fear into everyone. Bailey and everyone else continued on as if waiting for something dreadful they couldn't articulate. Bailey, remembering Talley's claim that students were members of the cult along with their parents, watched his classmates, wondering. He asked Talley what came next. No answer.

Wednesday night the phone rang during TV time and interrupted Bailey's thoughts. His mother answered and sounded very pleased when she told Bailey the call was for him. He was terrified to answer. He wondered if this was what it was like for criminals and people who lived with secrets. Every new interaction might open the secret door.

"Hello?" he said, sounding much more nervous than he was.

"Bailey? It's Brittany, from home room."

Already Bailey was suspicious. Last week, he wouldn't have believed his luck and sense of relief that a popular, pretty girl had called him. In his excitement, he forgot her role in his daily torment. Then, he wondered if the snake was about to pop out of the peanut can. Still, he was a sixteen-year-old boy, and a call from a pretty girl was a call from a pretty girl.

"Oh, hi."

"Hey, I just wanted to tell you I'm sorry about how I've acted," she said.

"It's okay."

"I heard about what you did to Teddy. Did you really break his hand?"

"No, it wasn't that bad."

Stories always get better in the retelling. But did she know the untold story?

"Well, everyone's talking about it," she said. "I mean, you're so different lately."

"Things have been weird," he said.

"Yeah, I know. That why I wanted to ask you to a party at my place."

"Tonight? On a Wednesday?"

"Just some friends and I. We want to take our minds off things. Would you like to come? It's sort of an outdoor, bonfire type of thing. My parents will be here. My dad can talk to your dad if you want."

Despite the inner warning light, Bailey wanted to go. With Talley gone quiet, maybe for good, this was a hand up, a way out of his low status. If this was what assertiveness got a man, he would develop his own, apart from Talley.

"Sure, I'd like to go. Just let me check with my parents."

Bailey told his parents about the invitation and asked their permission. It surprised them that a rich girl had asked him to a party.

"You sure this is on the up and up?" Roger asked.

"Why wouldn't it be?" his mother asked.

"It's Wednesday night," Roger said. "Not the usual party night."

"It's just a last-minute get-together," Bailey said.

His father looked Bailey hard in the eyes to make sure they understood each other.

"I think it's the real deal," Bailey said.

His parents discussed it. Bailey waited, anguished at keeping Brittany waiting. They gave their assent, and he told her he was coming. He hung up the phone and put on his coat.

"You're wearing that shirt again?" his father asked. "Maybe you should switch it up a little and give it the night off."

"I like it," Bailey said. "It's my favorite shirt. I feel good in it."

He was relieved when his parents declined to press the issue. The only caveat was that Roger had to drive him there. With the recent disappearances, Bailey's father would not bend an inch. They compromised, and Roger agreed to let his son off a block away.

Bailey jogged to Brittany's house. It was in a new development on the edge of town, surrounded by the woods. He'd never been to a party like this. Did this mean he was a cool kid? His troubled mind calmed. He hoped his worries would fade.

The house looked quiet when he arrived. He cursed himself for being the first one there. That was embarrassing. On the bright side, he'd get a few minutes alone with Brittany. He felt an electric surge through his arms at that thought. He rang the doorbell and waited. After a few seconds, he couldn't resist a peek through the sidelight windows. He saw Brittany coming toward the front door. His heart jumped. The house was dark.

Brittany let him into the house. She was friendly and seemed happy he had come.

"Don't take off your coat," she said. "I need you to help me start the bonfire."

She led him through the house to the back door as she put on her coat. He had never been in a house so nice. It was empty and still. He expected to meet her parents, who would look at him with scorn or pity or both, but he saw no one.

They went outside. He followed her through the snow and they continued toward the trees. In the middle of the vast backyard, she gave him matches. He lit a pile of logs. For a moment, he stood transfixed, watching the roaring fire and enjoying its warmth. He also enjoyed her presence next to him. They sat on a bench together. She leaned into him. It was a new world.

Part of him wondered what had brought on this new attention from the popular girl. His first instinct was suspicion. But things had changed. He had dropped Teddy to his knees. She didn't know about Todd, he hoped, but she had to feel the new energy he radiated. He had a new strength. She sensed it and was attracted to it.

Question was: Now what? He'd never been in this position. Was this the part where he steals a kiss?

They're coming.

What a time for Arthur Talley to reassert himself. Bailey jumped as if stabbed.

"What's wrong," Brittany asked.

"Nothing," he said. "Just got a chill."

Now's the time to finish what we've started.

With her? I will not hurt her.

She's one of them. Remember how she treated you?

It's different now.

Because of me.

I still won't hurt her.

Just do what needs to be done. If she survives, you can make any play on her you want.

"Who let the loser in?"

A familiar voice cut through dark silence. Bailey jumped to his feet.

Teddy and his remaining henchman, Willy, came into the firelight. Bailey tensed and clenched his fists. He looked at Brittany and saw malevolent betrayal in her eyes. Talley's derisive laughter echoed in Bailey's head.

Willy was bigger than Todd. He came toward Bailey. Brittany stood and joined Teddy. Everyone glared at Bailey with looks of boiling hatred. Bailey shook his head, exhausted.

"Why do you hate me?" he asked.

"Because you're a loser," Teddy said.

Bailey nodded. "If you're a winner, Teddy, I don't want to be one."

Teddy scowled and looked at Willy. "Make it hurt."

"Why don't you make it hurt, Teddy?" Bailey asked.

"And make it slow," Teddy said to Willy.

"Where's Todd?" Bailey asked with a grin.

Willy froze. He looked back at Teddy, who shared a look with Brittany.

"You know something?" Brittany asked.

Bailey shrugged.

"Hell with this," Teddy said. "Willy, take him out so we can get our party going."

Surrender.

Bailey surrendered his body. Willy closed the distance. Bailey sensed the bloodlust of everyone around him.

Despite his size advantage, Willy was no match for the ferocity dwelling Bailey's mind and body. Bailey picked up a burning log, swung it upwards, and tagged Willy hard on the chin. Willy fell to the ground, dazed. Bailey didn't hesitate. The burning log came up and down in glowing arcs like a fiery sword until the bully was dead. Bailey stood up straight and tossed the burning, bloody log at Teddy. Teddy caught the flaming branch and screamed when it seared his hands. He tossed it onto the snow and plunged his hands in after it.

Bailey rushed the little thug, grabbed him by the coat, and dragged him to the bonfire.

Brittany looked into the woods.

"What are you waiting for???" she screamed. "Do something!"

Bailey tossed Teddy on the fire. Teddy thrashed and screamed in panic. He tried to escape the fire, but Bailey had another burning log, and pummeled Teddy with it, keeping him trapped in the fire. Bailey's face remained stone as the other screamed in panic and pain.

Brittany continued to scream for help until Teddy was dead in the fire. Bailey turned to face Brittany. She backed away at the look in his eyes.

"Tell them to come out," Bailey heard himself say.

She looked around, shaking and terrified.

Bailey turned in a circle as he spoke. "Come out!"

One by one, shadows came out of the trees and into the light. Bailey braced himself for monsters or demons. But it was only people. Seven of them. Adults. Most of them he recognized, including Brittany's parents. A couple of them were large men.

I can't take them, Bailey thought.

Just let them do what they're going to do. Trust me.

Brittany stood arrogant again in the safety of the adults. Bailey swallowed hard.

"Are you going to kill me?"

The tallest man, Mr. Sindor, his Geometry teacher, stepped forward.

"We were curious about you, Bailey," he said. "I saw Todd chase after you when school ended. On the day he vanished. Do you remember?"

"Yeah."

"We found his body," Sindor said. "It was in the ravine. But you knew that."

Bailey nodded. Brittany was shocked.

"And now you've killed Willy and Teddy," Sindor said. "Impressive you could kill your tormentors, especially considering the size disadvantage and that they outnumbered you."

Bailey was quiet.

"Is it just puberty?" Sindor asked. "Some kind of hormonal surge transforming you into a man of power like your father?"

Bailey remained quiet.

"Could be, but I suspect something more," Sindor said. "Care to tell us what's going on?"

"No."

"Very well," Sindor said. "But we like what we see. You're going to come with us. You'll have a choice to make. But rather than tell you, we'll show you."

Sindor turned to the others. "Bring him."

Don't fight them.

Bailey offered no resistance as the group pulled him along and bundled him into a van. Brittany sat next to him in the middle bench. She stared at him, unsure what to think of him.

The van pulled away from Brittany's house and drove away. No one noticed the flatbed truck with the homemade wood side panels. After a few seconds, the truck followed.

It was no surprise to Bailey when the van took them to the school-house. He could have led them to the tunnel entrance by the big tree in the woods, could have led them down the staircase and into the old buried schoolhouse. He knew where they were going, but he feigned ignorance.

Surprise came not for Bailey, but for the others when they entered the temple with enough flashlights to illuminate the cavern.

"What is this?" Sindor shouted.

He was the loudest of everyone, for they all shouted in surprise and shock. The six missing townspeople were gagged, tied, and hanging by their armpits from the bottom of the wooden bridge over the yawning chasm. Four were unconscious. The other two, barely awake. They had gone missing Saturday night and had been tied up for four days. Sindor and the others turned to Bailey.

"You did this?" he asked.

Bailey grinned and nodded. Talley answered. "Yes, I did this. And you and them brought innocent men, women, and children here to feed to the eel. You and your ancestors. It's been going on for centuries. Am I right?"

Brittany backed away from the scene, toward the opening. She was the only one of the group who felt any portent of danger.

Sindor shoved Bailey to the ground as the group rushed to the bridge. They talked over each other as they tried to figure out how to rescue their fellow group members hanging below. They got on their knees and worked together to pull them up.

Brittany stood by the temple portico. She sensed she might need to run.

Bailey got to his feet.

"You're a dead man!" Sindor shouted at him.

They had the first person pulled up to the bridge.

Bailey walked behind the altar. Brittany watched. He picked up a battered, green Army bag and fished out a Zippo lighter. He walked to the base of the bridge, flicked on the lighter, and dropped it on the wood.

The smell of death and rot was so strong in the chamber the group couldn't smell the lighter fluid soaking the bridge. Fire roared to life on each side of the hole and on the handrails. The bridge's center was untreated. The cult huddled in the center, all of them screaming and cursing that Bailey had outsmarted them.

Fire burned through the ropes, and the remaining five people hanging from the bridge plummeted into the abyss. Only one of them was awake when she fell. Her screams faded with her descent.

The cult tried to figure out how to escape the flames, but the fire blocked their exit, and the only way out was down.

Bailey stood next to the burning bridge and laughed. Brittany turned to run, but someone blocked her way. It was Roger, a shotgun in his hands.

A tremor shook the ground and walls.

"It waking up!" Bailey yelled. Talley was in full control now.

Roger watched his son in shock.

"You gave me your word you'd care for my mother!" Talley yelled.

The cult members frowned despite their panic. Sindor caught the meaning and understood what was going on with Bailey. He sputtered to explain himself and the others.

Brittany tried to flee, but Roger pinned her against the wall.

"What's going on?" he asked. "Bailey!"

Bailey wasn't able to recognize his father's voice.

The ground shook harder and a fetid, hissing wind came from the hole. Panic reached madness level for the cult as the giant eel's head rose from the hole. It was a dark gray, glob-like mass with white, unseeing eyes. They screamed as the creature opened its jagged jaws. It burst through the burning bridge and drew them all in at once.

Brittany looked away from the awful sight. Roger stared frozen in shock. Talley watched through Bailey's eyes with malevolent glee as the monster gulped his enemies with a series of terrible convulsions.

When the cult was gone, the creature thrashed its head in distress.

Roger turned to Brittany. "What's wrong?"

Brittany's mind had gone to another place. Roger ran down to the main floor of the temple.

Bailey watched the monster, curious. Roger came to Bailey's side and studied him.

"Bailey?"

Bailey looked at Roger, who didn't recognize the expression on his son's face.

The creature groaned as its thrashing grew weaker. Finally, its mammoth head slammed into the ground. It let out a final, horrid, breath. Then slowly, the weight of the dead creature's body drew it into the chasm. It rumbled down the hole until it crashed to the bottom far below. Silence remained.

"It choked on 'em," Roger said. "Didn't it?"

"Usually they feed it one person at a time," Bailey said. "I let it bite off more than it could chew."

The boy chuckled in a manner so sinister Roger knew something had taken over.

"Who are you?" he asked. "Where's my boy? Is he in there?"

Bailey backhanded Roger. He fell down hard, dazed by the surprise blow. Bailey rushed past him, his eyes on Brittany.

The girl screamed and ran for the entrance. Bailey caught her as she dove through. He pulled her back and threw her to the ground. From his belt he pulled a long knife.

"You're the last loose end," Bailey said.

"Stop!"

Bailey looked up to see Roger aiming the shotgun at him.

"You're not going to shoot your own son," Bailey said.

He turned his attention back to Brittany, ready to finish her.

"Is Bailey gone?" Roger asked.

Bailey hesitated.

"If he's gone, then there's reason not to shoot you," Roger said.

Bailey growled.

"Son, fight your way out," Roger said.

54

Keep me with you. You'll be powerful!
Bailey turned away from Brittany and came at Roger with the knife held high. Roger raised the rifle and aimed.

"Bailey! Come out!"

Kill him! He's a poor man!

You promised me you'd leave when you got them back, Bailey thought.

Let's be free. Take the girl for your own!

Roger put his finger on the trigger. Bailey froze. He doubled over and dropped the knife.

"Fight, son! Fight!"

The old man can teach you nothing. You're weak! Think of how far I'll take you!

He taught me everything, Bailey thought. And I'll make my own way!

He fell to the ground and rolled onto his back.

"Take . . . the shirt," he said.

Roger frowned for a second, then understood. He dropped the shotgun and tore Bailey's shirt open. Talley reasserted himself with a final primal burst of blind fury. Roger had to fight to get the shirt off. It took all of his strength to overpower Talley's essence. He tore the shirt to ribbons. Bailey screamed. Talley was forced from his mind and spirit for good. Roger got the shirt off his son's back. When Bailey was free of the shirt, he relaxed and caught his breath.

Roger stood over him, holding the shirt. A mass of fallen flashlights gave off odd angles of light.

"Bailey? You back?" he asked.

Bailey nodded. "Burn it. Quick."

Roger walked to the hole. The support posts standing at the foot of the bridge still burned. He tossed the fabric onto the flames and watched it burn. A haunting wail rose from the burning shirt. It grew louder and flowed across the temple chamber like a ghostly wind. When the shirt was ashes, the tortured voice was silent.

Bailey was back to his feet. Roger went to him and covered him with his coat. They walked out of the temple. As they did, they found Brittany standing by the door. She looked lost.

"My parents are dead," she said.

Roger was about to express sympathy, but Bailey spoke first.

"You were one of them," he said to Brittany. "You should have gone down with them."

It puzzled Roger. He didn't recognize anything about his son in the moment. Brittany shook where she stood, certain she was a dead woman.

"I don't care what you tell the police," Bailey said. "But leave us out of it. He told me everything, things you don't even know."

She nodded. "What will I do now?"

"Their spirits will come for you unless you turn away," Bailey said. "Come see us if you want a new start. An honest one."

Bailey left. Roger hesitated, but trusted Bailey's judgment and followed. He handed the girl a flashlight. Brittany was alone in the temple chamber.

Roger drove away from the school. Sindor's van was still in the lot. Bailey was numb from the ordeal.

"That was weird," Bailey said.

Roger looked at him, then both men burst into laughter, exorcising their pent-up stress.

"What do we do now?" Bailey asked. "How do we live knowing things like that are out there?"

Roger thought about it. "They've always been out there. We've been warned since the Old Testament not to meddle in those powers. It's just another lesson learned, you ask me."

"But there's a greater power, right?" Bailey asked.

Roger looked at Bailey and smiled. "We won, didn't we?"

Bailey nodded. "I guess we did."

They drove the rest of the way home in silence.

Mr. Cold

Sawyer was a little North Dakota village of three hundred people where it was cold most of the year. It was the first stop from nowhere, or the last to nowhere, depending on your direction. Either way, it was a place to refuel, get a meal, and pass through. Most of the small businesses catered to this passing-through clientele. It was so far out of the way that no one noticed the strange happenings until it was too late.

The hamlet faded into view as Sheriff Howard steered the rumbling snowcat through the winter storm. The afternoon to evening transition cast the village in an eerie, bluish haze. Scattered street lamps were lit, although they looked like fairies in the swirling snow. Sheriff Howard sensed an empty stillness and was uneasy. Cop hunch, perhaps. He got the same vibe from his two deputies riding with him.

The sheriff turned to Trevor, who sat next to him.

"Try again," Howard said.

The deputy tapped on the screen of his smartphone, held it to his ear, and waited.

The snowcat inched forward, passing the snow-covered speed limit sign that Howard knew ordered drivers to slow to 25 miles-per-hour for town driving. They entered downtown. Howard was grateful for the heated cab. The 1980s vintage tracked vehicle had been a gift to the department. Being enclosed in the warmth, watching the snow beat around them, reflecting the blue and red of the police lights, gave Howard the feeling of being in a spaceship on an alien world.

"No answer," Trevor said.

"Got a signal?" Howard asked.

"Signal's good," Trevor said. "It ain't the phone. No one's answering."

"Dotty's should still be open," said Tom, from the back seat.

Howard glanced at Trevor, who called the number for Dotty's Diner.

The sheriff scanned the empty streets for some sign of trouble as Trevor waited for an answer. He knew what the result would be as Trevor shook his head and ended the call.

"No answer at Dotty's house or at her diner."

"A little early for everyone to be in bed asleep," Tom said.

"We'll go to Dotty's," Howard said. "If there's trouble, people would go there."

Dotty's Diner was midway down Main Street. As expected, there were several cars parked at an angle on the fronting curb.

"If she's open, I'm having a Reuben," Trevor said.

Everyone nodded and added their own choices from the menu.

"What is that?" Howard asked, pointed ahead and to the left.

A white object stood on the sidewalk outside the grocery. Hard to see in the driving snow.

"Something white," Trevor said.

"Some kind of snow pile?" Tom asked.

"Looks more like a column," Howard said.

"Of snow?" Trevor asked.

Howard shrugged and navigated toward the object. The men pulled up their hoods and bundled up.

They piled out into the cold. Everyone clenched up as the brutal icy wind slammed against them, as if they were invaders under attack. Thick snowflakes patted against their goggles, making visibility difficult. They trudged toward the object. Leaning in close for a better inspection, Howard's eyes went wide.

"Oh, my God!" Tom said.

"It's a person!" Trevor said.

There was no denying it was a man, frozen in the place where he stood. He had a six-inch layer of snow on his windward side. The deputies rushed forward. They had to high-step through the drifting snow. Howard put his hand on the man's shoulder.

"He's frozen stiff!" he said.

Trevor brushed off the snow from the man's head. Howard stepped in for a closer look. On the side uncovered by snow, Howard ran his gloved hand over a thin layer of sparkling frost. He removed his glove and did his best to check for a pulse on the man's neck and wrist. In seconds, he had to put his glove back on.

"Too cold for that," he said. "Don't know how I would check a pulse, anyway. He's covered in ice."

"Perfectly covered," Tom said. "It's not thick ice here and thin there. It's the same thickness all over his body."

"Who is it?" Trevor asked.

"Judging by the nose, I'd say it's Lewis Trilby," Howard said. "We're outside his store."

"Look how he's positioned," Tom said. "Looks like he was running."

"He's not wearing a coat," Trevor said.

"His hand is on the post here," Howard said. "Otherwise he'd fall over. He froze in seconds."

"Is it that cold out?" Tom asked.

"It's cold, but not that cold," Howard said.

"Could be a sudden thing," Trevor said. "Something like this happened in Illinois in the 1800s."

"So . . . now what?" Tom asked.

Howard studied the frozen man. "I'm afraid if we move him we might break a damn limb off."

"Could a person survive this?" Trevor asked.

Howard nodded. "It's happened. A sudden cold comes and the body's systems shut down. Think about pressing the pause button on your VCR."

"You still have a VCR, boss?" Tom asked.

"Focus, please," Howard said.

"Maybe we should get him inside and try to thaw him out. See what happens," Tom said.

Howard thought about that. "How long ago did we start getting calls about Sawyer?"

"Hour and a half ago," Trevor said. "Same time those UFO calls came in."

"So it's been ninety minutes since friends and family of the Sawyer folks started noticing they weren't answering calls and such," Howard said. "So whatever happened here probably started at least two hours ago."

He looked at Lewis Trilby. "Well, if he's been frozen this long, he'll either make it or he won't. If he's dead, he's dead. If he's paused, he'll stay paused until we can think of something. Let's check out the rest of the village."

They returned to the snowcat. Howard eased it forward as the others removed their gloves and masks and relaxed in the warmth.

"Trevor, shine that light around," Howard said.

Trevor gripped the interior handle of the outside spotlight and swept its beam across Main Street.

"Boss!" he yelled.

Howard stopped just in time to avoid hitting another frozen person.

"I'll be damned! Another one!" Tom said as they bundled up again.

They gathered around the new frozen figure. It was a woman.

"It's Dotty," Trevor said. "You can tell because of her—"

A glare from Howard.

"Well, you can just tell," Trevor said.

"Look!" Tom said, pointing.

There were four more frozen people. All of them, like Dotty, had froze in the act of running.

"They were coming out of Dotty's Diner," Howard said. "All of them frozen on the spot."

The three men left the warmth and walked into the diner. They checked the other frozen victims for some sign of life or consciousness. They had to squeeze past a man standing in the door to enter the diner. When they were through, the three of them stood in silent shock.

"I can't believe this," Trevor said.

The diner was in a state of panic. Patrons and employees were in various states of rising, running, and falling. Faces were masks of surprise and panic. Food was stuck to the plates. A coffee cup sat in mid-air. Its frosted contents trailed down in a mahogany icicle, rooted to a frosty puddle on the floor.

"Just like you said, Boss," Tom said. "A pause button."

Trevor took off his gloves. "It's warm in here. The heat's still working."

The others took off their gloves, masks, and hoods. Howard nodded.

"So why aren't they melting?" he asked.

He walked to the nearest booth, where a family of four sat frozen, staring at the door in terror. Howard ran his bare hands along the frost that covered them.

"Cold as the outdoors," he said. "It's a different cold, I guess. But how?"

"This don't make any sense," Tom said.

"I'm creeped out, Boss," Trevor said. "Let's call the state police."

"Not so fast," Howard said. "Let's check a few houses first. Dotty's and Trilby's store would be the only places open when this happened. Anyone else would be at home. Let's see if anyone escaped whatever happened."

"Should we split up?" Trevor asked.

"We'll stay together," Howard said.

The men left Dotty's and got back into the snowcat. They had traveled two blocks when they encountered another group of people frozen in mid-run.

"What's this now?" Howard asked.

"They're running from the church," Trevor said. "They were at

61

mass. Two hours ago."

"There's our timeline," Tom said. "Two hours ago this hit."

"I didn't think about church being in session," Howard said.

"Because you're a heathen, Boss," Trevor said.

"Not anymore," Howard said.

They couldn't continue on without hitting people in the street, so they got out and checked the them for any sign of life before walking the final three blocks into the residential area. They walked up the side-walk of the first house they came to. Howard knocked. They didn't expect an answer and didn't get one. Inside, they found an elderly couple iced over in their easy chairs. He, reading the paper. She, doing some knitting. A dying fire flickered in the hearth.

"Fire's going," Trevor said. "Interesting."

The next three houses had similar scenes, with men, women, and children captured in what Trevor started calling the "ice pause." At the fourth house, they had to search around until they found the occupants.

"In here!" Tom called.

The others went upstairs to find Tom standing in the doorway to the bathroom. Inside was a young couple. He was at the sink, shaving cream crystallized to his half-shaved face. He shrank away from the door as if an intruder had entered at the moment he froze. His wife had been rising from the bathtub when the freeze hit her. Her hand was on the edge of the tub, and she was halfway to a standing position. Streams of glittering, frozen water descended from her body. The bath water had frozen in mid-wave. The humidity generated by their evening bath had left a frost on the walls and floor.

"I think we get the idea, fellas," Howard said. "Let's get back to the cat and call the state police."

They left the house and trudged to the sidewalk. There, Trevor spotted something different.

"Check it out, Boss."

The snow had lightened enough for them to see another figure a block further on.

"Something's different about that one," Trevor said.

"Let's go," Howard said.

As they drew near, it was clear that it wasn't human.

"Holy cow, it's empty!" Tom said.

They arrived to find the ice shaped like a person, but with no person inside of it. The front was there, the back was broken away and missing.

"Looks like a damn cicada shell in the summertime!" Howard said.

Trevor walked around behind the ice shell.

"There's blood!"

The other two rushed around to see Trevor pointing at a splash of blood where the neck would have been. Further examination showed patches of pink tissue in the arms of the shell.

"Is that skin?" Tom asked. His voice shook.

Howard leaned in close. "It's skin, all right. Poor bastard got injured somehow. He got away from the freeze, but left some of his skin when he did."

"That's not all," Trevor said. "Look at those little sharp points. Little ice daggers."

Thin ice shards dotted the inside of the shell like an iron maiden. Frozen blood drops covered the tips. Another blue substance dripped from the ice. Trevor leaned in close to inspect the shards.

"They're hollow. What do you make of that?" Trevor asked.

"We have a strange substance that looks like ice, but isn't," Howard said, thinking about what they had discovered. "It freezes people instantly in a shell."

"And the shell has needles that inject them with whatever that blue gunk is," Tom said.

"What does the blue gunk do to them?" Howard asked.

"So we absolutely get the troopers in now," Tom said.

"No, we have an injured man out there who needs help," Howard said. "Let's see if we can find him."

Tom didn't care for that idea, but he nodded his agreement.

"Let's see if there's a blood trail," Howard said. "Anything?"

The deputies said no, they didn't see any blood.

"I got footprints," Tom said.

The footprints were filled with falling snow, but there remained enough of a depression to see them.

"They lead off into the park," Trevor said.

They followed the tracks through the deep snow. Their legs wobbled from the constant strain. Darkness overtook them as they reached the edge of the park. Tom looked back to the lights of Main Street and the twirling color of the snowcat's lights. He longed to be in its warm cab again.

"HELLO!" Howard shouted.

The deputies jumped at the sound. The greeting echoed into the murky snow and wind.

"This is the sheriff! If you're injured and need help, call out if you can!"

Howard gestured at the deputies to be quiet so they could listen. Nothing.

He turned to his men. "Okay—"

A sharp growl sounded from the hidden depths of the park.

"You guys hear that?" Tom asked, panicking.

"Take it easy, Tom. Probably just a scared dog," Howard said.

"We've only seen frozen dogs and cats," Tom said. "I'm going back to the—"

Howard seized Tom by the collar. "You're going to do your duty, Deputy!"

Tom relaxed a little and nodded.

"I'm scared as hell, too, fellas," Howard said. "But this is why we took the oath. Now, we're gonna search this park. Someone's hurt and might be seconds away from dying. And there might be big trouble, too, so be ready to draw if you need to. But only if you need to. Other-wise, keep your weapons inside your coat where they'll be warm. You boys keep your guns dry, don't you?"

The men nodded.

"Good. Let's move out and stay together."

It was just a small town park with benches and trees and playground equipment. A statue of a long-ago war hero stood in the center square. But something was different. The three lawmen entered the park grounds with bodies wound tight with anxiety. The trees, so beautiful in the spring and summer, now looked threatening. The swings and monkey bars rose from the snow like the ruins of alien cities.

"The snow's churned up by the water fountain," Trevor said. "Look."

Everyone stopped moving as they watched the area around the fountain. Sheriff Howard called out again. Again he got silence in reply. A blur of movement darted away from the fountain. The men jumped.

"Stop! Sheriff!" Howard yelled.

He ran after the source of the movement as fast as the thick snow would let him. The two younger deputies bounded past him, their youthful legs carrying them over the drifts.

It was a man. Of that they were sure. He ran between trees, trying to lose them. He wore no coat, and his clothes were bloody. Howard continued to call out to him, alternating between barking orders and offering to help. They passed two more humanoid ice shells. Like the first one, they were empty and stained with blood. The snow around them was disturbed led away from them.

The pursuit took them through the park and to the far side. There, the officers stopped as they came upon a new, unbelievable sight. A cluster of frozen people lined the sidewalk in front of a row of houses. The front doors of those houses were open. Howard put it together right away. Neighbors had gathered outside to discuss whatever was happening, and the freeze had hit them all at once.

"Step away, now!" Trevor yelled.

Howard tried to focus on whatever Trevor had seen.

The man they chased was next to a frozen woman. His mouth was at her neck. His head shook back and forth like a leopard with its prey. Howard had seen enough. He drew his weapon.

"Step away from her!" he shouted. "This is your only warning!"

The man didn't even look back. Howard sidestepped to get an angle that wouldn't send a bullet through any of the frozen people and fired. The shot exploded into the peaceful night, and the round went through the man's back. It spun him, but he didn't fall down. Finally, noticing the officers, he faced them and roared. Six inch fangs sprouted out of his gums.

"Oh, damn," Howard said.

The man ran towards them as the deputies drew their weapons. All three opened fired on the man, who fell dead after absorbing ten rounds.

After catching their breath, they ran the ten feet of distance to examine the body. Trevor turned him over.

"It's Doc Lowry," Howard said. "Or it was. Something changed him."

"No, we know what the blue gunk does, I'll bet," Trevor said.

"I think so, yes," Howard said.

"He's almost completely white," Trevor said. "Not a drop of blood in him.

"So the town doctor is dead," Tom said.

"I know where you're going with this, Tom, and I agree," Howard said. "Let's get to the 'cat and call the state police. We're outclassed here."

The trudged back toward the snowcat. Halfway through the park, they had to stop again. Nobody had to point it out. They all saw it.

A dozen or more people staggered toward them from Main Street, Lewis Trilby and Dotty among them. Howard looked back. The folks from the neighborhood also advanced. All of them were free of their ice shells and sported fangs too large for their mouths.

"How can we shoot them all?" Tom asked.

"It took, what, ten shots just to take down the doc?" Trevor asked.

"We don't have enough ammo for that many shots."

"Our only hope is the snowcat," Howard said. "We just have to do our best. You fellas are younger and faster. If I don't make it, get your asses out of here."

"Let's make our shots count," Trevor said. "Go for the head."

"Right," Tom said.

The men moved forward, glancing back to see how fast the neighborhood people closed in. They moved slowly at first, but developed a speed and agility that allowed them to move through the snow much faster than the officers. The mutants surrounded them and relentlessly closed in.

"We're boxed in," Howard said. "Last stand, I guess."

"I'm saving a bullet for me," Tom said.

The others glanced at him but said nothing.

The creatures growled and licked their lips and new fangs. Their eyes were blank as the ice that covered their skin.

"Well, I'm not gonna stand here and wait to die," Howard said. "Let's make a run for it."

As they flexed to run, a hard blast of frigid air hit them from behind. The force drove all three of them face-first into the snow. They scrambled to their feet, dazed and puzzled. The monsters, people they once knew, were closer, and their eyes were full of murder.

"The hell was that?" Trevor asked as the wind hit again.

Again it knocked them over.

"That damn wind!" Tom said. "I can feel the cold through my parka!"

"Must be the wind that froze them," Howard said.

"And changed them," Trevor added.

"We need shelter," Howard said.

He looked around. "We're still closer to the houses. That might be our best bet. Wait it out 'til morning."

"You're forgetting that the cold went inside the houses, too," Tom said. "We won't be safe there."

"Our winter clothing is keeping us safe for now," Howard said. "Maybe we can hold out."

"Look out!" Tom shouted.

The ring of creatures had doubled, and they were moving fast.

"We're out of time," Trevor said.

Howard glanced at him, surprised at his calm.

"Let's get up that hill!" Tom said.

They looked to where he pointed. A tall mound of snow sat next to a giant oak tree. Tom ran to it. They followed.

"We can use the hill to get onto the tree," Tom said over his shoulder. "We'll have the high ground and can pick up off from above."

"I'm too old for that damn rigmarole," Howard said.

"Not a bad idea," Trevor said. "You can do it, Boss."

Howard grumbled as they ran through the snow with excruciating slowness. Tom reached the base of the hill and climbed. He was halfway up the hill when the snow beneath him gave way. Trevor ducked away as Tom slid down the hill and crashed back to the ground. Tom struggled to his feet and brushed off the snow. Another blast of freezing air pummeled them as Howard reached them.

Despite the incoming danger, Trevor wiped at the side of the snow mound with his arm.

"What the hell are you doing?" Tom asked.

Howard grabbed Trevor's parka to lead him away. "Come on!"

"It's pure ice. Look!" Trevor said.

Howard studied it close. Tom backed away.

"Okay, it's ice. Bravo. Now let's move it!" Tom said.

"Smooth as glass," Trevor said. "Looks like a giant ice cube."

He removed another layer of snow, revealing more of what hid beneath. A large slab of smooth ice faced them.

"This ain't a snow hill," Trevor said. 'It's an ice cube big as a house."

"It's a frozen meteor," Tom said. "Remember our UFO calls we got earlier? Here it is."

"This is the source of trouble, men," Howard said. "I'll bet on it."

"So these things are—" Tom said.

Trevor and Howard looked to see what made Tom shut up.

The creatures stopped advancing. They were only twenty feet away in a ring, cutting off their escape.

"Why'd they stop?" Tom asked.

"Because of this," Trevor said, tapping the ice mound.

He resumed brushing off the snow, and the others helped him. The creatures stirred in place, but didn't come closer.

"Sure is huge," Tom said.

"Quiet, Deputy," Howard said. "Nobody can think with your rat-a-tat-tat stating of the obvious."

"Sorry, Boss. Just nervous."

Howard brushed at a pile of snow and fell through an opening. The smooth wall of the mound had an entrance. Trevor and Tom gathered around Howard. They shined their flashlights into the entrance, revealing a tall, icy corridor that stretched into the darkness.

"When are we gonna wake up from this nightmare?" Tom asked.

Howard looked back at the creatures. They flailed their arms and roared at the night.

"It isn't any ol' chunk of ice, boss," Trevor said. "This was made by unseen hands. I don't want to know whose hands it was."

"Should we go in?" Tom asked. "Those things seem restrained for the moment."

The freezing wind buffeted them again. Howard nodded.

"We better get inside and take our chances," he said.

"The wind is coming from this thing," Trevor said. "You realize that, right?"

"We're out of options," Howard said. "But I can't give you orders in this circumstance. Stay or go. I'm going in."

With that, Howard walked into the corridor without looking back. Trevor looked at Tom, who shook his head.

"No way," Tom said. "I'll take my chances out here. These things are holding back."

"For now," Trevor said.

Tom was silent and didn't move. Trevor turned and entered the corridor.

He took a left and then a right turn, following a faint glow that grew in intensity as he followed it. He suspected Howard had done the same, and was proven right when he entered a chamber and found Howard standing next to an icy, rectangular box at least ten feet long. The sheriff stared into the box with a look of disbelief.

"What is it, boss?" Trevor asked, too frightened to join him and look for himself.

Howard, dazed, shook his head. "I don't know what to call it."

The only way to find out was to summon the courage and look, so Trevor joined Howard at the edge of the icy container to see what was inside.

It was humanoid and naked, although there was nothing to show male or female. Its skin was pure white. The enormous head was bald and framed by long, pointed ears. Long, sharp teeth, just like those of the transformed townspeople, protruded from its thin mouth and rested on its lower lip. Blood stained its teeth and lips. Wide eyes rested behind closed lids. It was still.

Both men stood silently, watching the thing and listening to their hurried breathing.

"Where's it from?" Howard asked, whispering. "Mars or Hell?"

"Damn thing's gotta be nine feet tall if he's a foot," Trevor said.

"Look at those teeth and claws. This is a predator, son. Like none we've ever seen."

"What now, Boss?" Trevor asked. "What now?"

"This is what started it all. This alien came here, froze the people, turned them into monsters and took their blood."

"Yeah?"

"And we're standing here staring at it like a couple of idiots."

"So the plan is to get as far away from it as we can," Trevor said.

"You're darn tootin'."

Howard ejected the magazine from his pistol and replaced it with a full one. Trevor did the same.

They heard Tom cry out from outside and spun around in the direction of the noise. A shuffle came from the icy sarcophagus and they turned again to see the creature rising to a sitting position. Its red eyes were wide and full of hate. Howard, closest and backing away, shoved Trevor toward the corridor.

"Go!"

The thing crawled out of the box as the men fled. It rose to its full intimidating height on thin, spindly legs. Trevor spared a look back as they rushed out of the room, seeing the look of stunned anger on the thing's face, as if it couldn't believe these lowly beings had reached its inner sanctum.

The men darted through the corridor, their hurried footsteps thudding on the floor as they scrambled out. Behind them, the lengthy stride of the invader followed with hard stomps.

They came out of the mound to find Tom under attack by the creatures. They tore at his parka and snow pants, as if they knew it gave him protection from the metamorphosing wind. He did his best to shoot them, but in his panic he fired blindly. One shot careened off the ice, inches from Howard's head.

Howard and Trevor opened fire on the creatures. They felled several of them, but it wasn't fast enough. The creatures pulled off his parka as the wind blew out of the ice mound and rocked Tom to the ground. Knowing what was happening, he got to his feet and tried to outrun it. The other two had no idea how to counter the attack .

The wind unleashed the freezing frost that spread over Tom's body as he screamed in terror. After two steps his legs were frozen in place. The frost traveled up his body. He growled in pain and fear.

"It's stabbing into me!" he shouted. "Shoot me! Dammit, shoot me!"

Trevor and Howard exchanged a glance. Trevor couldn't do it. Howard, his face grim, raised his pistol just as the creature came out of the ice mound and swept a long arm at Howard. The sheriff was thrown up and away a distance of five feet. He hit the side of the mound and rolled down. He dropped his weapon and clutched his arm, grimacing in pain. The thing swung again, but Trevor ducked and rolled. He was out of the thing's grasp. After getting to his feet, Trevor backpedaled away from the thing and its minions and was safe for the moment.

Tom was encased in ice. The thing looked at Howard, dismissed him as a threat, and turned its attention to Trevor. The creatures regrouped and formed a ring around him.

Trevor's mind spun. Tom was lost to the freeze and would soon be a creature like the others. Howard was unconscious at best, maybe already dead. He had enough shots left to take out a few of the creatures, but how effective the bullets would be. The closest shelter was the frozen thing's dwelling.

"Nothing but good options," Trevor said.

He decided if he was living his final night, he'd close it out by his own hand. He had a full clip in his belt.

"I'm counting the rounds," he said to the thing and its slaves. "Do you understand that? I'm going to count them so I make sure to save one for me."

The thing was near the entrance to the ice mound, blocking it. Trevor fired five rounds into the monster. It staggered back, waving at the air as if this was an unfamiliar experience. It was off guard, but the wounds didn't look fatal.

Tom, or what used to be Tom, broke free of his shell and rushed at Howard, who had yet to move. If Howard had survived the thing's attack, he wouldn't survive Tom's.

Trevor rushed past the bewildered monster and reentered the corridor. At the entrance, he emptied his weapon at them, taking out two more before his weapon clicked dry. He switched out the empty magazine for a new one as he ran back to the chamber. He heard the thing enter the corridor, roaring in anger as it regained its primitive sense of the hunt.

His mind went over all probable reasons and options, trying to apply what he knew against the fresh revelations about the higher world he didn't know existed. The thing was humanoid. Head shots worked. Maybe the thing's head—despite its clear resistance to bullets—was vulnerable.

He retreated to the chamber and waited. The weapon held fifteen rounds. Fourteen for the thing's head, one for Trevor's, if it came to that. Trevor slowed his breathing and aimed, nice and steady, at the space in the chamber entrance where the thing's head would appear. Its footsteps pounded closer, only a few feet away. Trevor held his breath.

It appeared in the entrance and Trevor opened fire.

"One! Two! Three!"

He called out each shot as they slammed into the thing's head. It stiffened up under the assault, making it easy for Trevor to send round after round into its head. After calling out the fourteenth shot, he paused to see how much damage he had inflicted. If this hadn't worked, he would have to shoot himself before the creature got to him.

The thing fell back against the wall. Its large red eyes rolled up until all that was visible was two huge, eerie orbs. It fell to the floor and began to deteriorate. Its skin shriveled and the blood it had consumed in its attack leaked from the body onto the floor. It was dead and decomposed. Trevor caught his breath and stared in disbelief. The climactic battle was over in seconds. He had lived.

The creatures were still out there, but Trevor guessed he could scare them off if he brought out their master's dead body. He had won. He was free.

The ice ship started to vibrate. Colored lights filled the opaque walls with rainbow color. The craft was about to take off for God knows where. Trevor decided that immediate escape was the better idea. He ran for the corridor, having trouble stepping over the thing's large, sprawling body. He felt a lurch like an elevator rising from the bottom floor. It caused him to lose his footing. After getting to his feet, he rushed through the corridor to see the entrance was closed. The door that had descended was clear thin ice. It was thin enough to see through, so he hoped it would be thin enough to break.

The craft shook harder, seconds from lift off. Another lurch fluttered his stomach, and he had the sick realization that the ice mound had lifted into the air. He looked at the pistol in his hand. One round left. He had saved it for himself, but what if the shot couldn't shatter the door and he was left to ride the craft to its destination?

He took a chance and fired at the door. The round penetrated the glass but didn't shatter it. A web of cracks spread out from the hold. Trevor stared at the damage in disbelief.

The craft rose into the air as the creatures reacted in panicked rage. Trevor saw them through the clear ice walls. Desperate, Trevor punched at the bullet hole. The cracks widened, but it was slow going. Too slow if he meant to escape. The snowy ground fell away. Trevor roared in anguish and drove his shoulder into the bullet hole. Again and again he pounded his weight into the door. His shoulder ached as he was sure he had dislocated it.

He was about to give up when the door shattered, and his momentum drove him out the entrance. It was a ten-foot fall, but cushioned by the snow. The craft rose above him. Trevor rolled over onto his back and watched it ascend, hardly able to believe he had escaped.

The creatures went wild with malevolent fury. In a primal sense, they knew he had defeated their master's plan. They fell upon each other, enraged. For the moment, they weren't interested in Trevor.

Thankful his shoulder was hurt and not his legs, he got to his feet and rode a surge of renewed adrenaline as he ran through the park, down the main street to the snowcat. Empty ice shells lined the streets and filled the cafe.

He crawled into the warm cab. It still idled. He put it in reverse and backed away. The creatures remembered their hunt, and regrouped to chase him. They caught up to the slow-moving machine. They pounded at the door and punched at the glass. Without their master, the attack was unfocused and weak.

The further he got from town, the more half-hearted their assault became. Trevor thought any power or intelligence they had was tied to the ice ship. He didn't know and was done caring. His shoulder throbbed in pain and kept him awake. He turned around and drove forward, away from the lights of Sawyer.

With the vehicle moving ahead steady, he radioed the state police. A panicked voice answered. No, they had no one to spare to come to Sawyer. Something strange was happening. Giant ice boulders had fallen all over the state. They must have come from outer space. Some sort of virus must have come with them. Everywhere the strange meteors had landed, the people were going insane.

Get home and stay there, the voice on the radio told him. The army would be called in for sure.

Trevor turned off the radio and sighed. He checked the gas gauge. Nowhere near enough to make it to South Dakota, but he decided to go south as far as he could. His family was from Oklahoma, so there was no one up here for him to save. He had only himself to look after.

He did his best to make his shoulder comfortable. Another full magazine was in the lockbox. He slid it into his weapon.

He would have to remember to count his rounds, just in case he needed to save the last one.

Shrine of the Possessing Rain

I distrusted this planet from the moment I saw it as just another glowing star in space. My ship's instruments identified it as my destination. For days it sat in the center of my viewing window. It grew larger as time passed by. It troubled my waking thoughts and disturbed my dreams when I slept. My inner voice told me to stay away, that this was one job I should not, could not accept.

Disagreements with the inner voice, though, were part of my job. When you court danger, face the unknowable and unexplainable, your mind and spirit rebels against the task. It's an instinct you never lose, even if you want to. Not only that, I am paid—as many a jittery client reminds me—to face that which most others cannot.

At first, things progressed as usual, which means I spend lots of time in-between jobs before a request comes in. I spend that time resting my spirit and filling my mind with knowledge. In my line of work, knowledge is a weapon, as is a rested and courageous spirit.

A message came through on a special communication device. It was from a client I had never heard of. I am the person called in when things are going wrong, when the practical men with tools of measurement and science are out of answers. They don't like to admit they're clueless, so it is often a high-ranking official who calls in a strange one like me. These bigwigs, understand, don't care whether the spirit world is real. It matters not an extra penny or less to them. What matters is results, and I have built my reputation on getting results.

The journey was long. Three quadrants from my home planet. A deadly phenomenon needed to be dealt with. Twelve workers dead via inconclusive means suggesting otherworldly influence. High risk and high travel meant much higher pay. I communicated this to the potential client. They agreed to my lofty price right away.

My ship is small and fast. All I pack for any job is fresh clothing, adequate food and water, and my medallion.

The medallion is a large gold disc centered with a white gemstone. The disc is fixed to a wide leather bracelet that never leaves my arm. It is through this medallion my group—The Brotherhood of the Word—can access the vast, forbidden Library of the Ages. To touch the gemstone and focus one's mind is to access lost knowledge from a spectral place in the higher realms. It's a physically and spiritually draining process. Only a select few can do it. The gemstone is only a gateway. One does not use the medallion carelessly.

I never guessed I would settle into a career of confronting phantom dangers, but not only did I make a handsome living from such risks, it was an inherited ability that allowed me to do so.

My father had the ability to access the Library of the Ages with the gemstone. He taught me the ways of the Brotherhood when it was clear I had inherited the special touch. He told me of incomprehensible dangers he had faced. His stories were terrifying. But he did well at his job, lived a long life, and died peacefully in his bed. It was our lot to put our souls at risk. A man does what his creator has designed him to do. I came around to my father's ideals because I tried making a living at other things and was neither happy nor satisfied. I'm not happy doing what I do, but I get satisfaction and a sense of contentment from it.

With that in mind, I accepted the offer, packed my bags, readied my ship, and set out on the two weeks journey. The flight was uneventful. My trips through space were infrequent enough that I never lost the wonder of flying through the stars. I got a sinking feeling when Velus became visible.

Soon I was close enough to contact my client. They gave me coordinates to the landing site. I made the rough descent into the atmosphere and found plenty of vibrant beauty. Oceans and jungles and forests passed beneath the hull of my little craft. There were lands of such beauty I ached to stop and have a walk around.

My destination, however, was nowhere near so beautiful. My guides directed me along a path that saw trees, grass, and rivers give way to a place of grayness and darkness. A desert of ashes was how it appeared. There was dank fog. Dust blew through the air. I had to fly with instruments. My visibility was nowhere near adequate.

Soaring ruins of unknown construction and age appeared out of the gloom. I flew over a high stone wall. From my vantage point, it looked older than any structure I had seen across the galaxy. Squat stone buildings passed below. Nowhere did I see people walking its streets or going back and forth from its buildings and houses. The further I flew into the city, the more tall and spaced apart the structures became.

I followed instructions and landed in a sheltered courtyard appropriated for ship landings. It was quite a contrast to see modern ships, vehicles, and equipment scattered about an abandoned city as old as time. Workers buzzed about. A variety of terrestrial craft crisscrossed the sky. It was a busy scene. A modern base of operations that stood out against the ancientness of its surroundings.

I got out of my craft. Two men left a waiting hovercraft to meet me.

"Mr. Biringer?" the taller one asked.

"That's me," I said.

"I'm Turus. Thank you for coming."

"Thank you for thinking of me."

"This is Dubbs," Turus said, indicating the man next to him.

We exchanged pleasantries as Turus led us off the courtyard to a waiting hovercraft. He started the vehicle, and we were off. I barely got situated in time.

"Looks busy," I said, referring to the workers running and flying about.

"For now," Turus said. "We still have some work to finish. But unless we can get this situation with the tower cleared up, we'll come to a complete halt. That's why you're here. I hope you're worth the money."

"I assume you're the man in charge?" I said.

"The one and only."

"So what can you tell me about Velus?" I asked.

"First of all, we're not sure what the planet's proper name is, if it has one," Turus said. "If you'll remember, astronomers from the home world discovered Velus two hundred years ago. Velus is the name they gave it."

"Fascinating," I said.

I knew all of this, but had forgotten.

"Obviously, someone lived here long ago," Turus said. "Thousands of years ago, by our preliminary estimate. If they had a name for this rock, we haven't found it yet."

"They left no written works that we've found," Dubbs said. "Lots of pictures and symbols. We're trying to decipher it all. Totally unknown stuff. Pretty exciting, all things considered."

"How long have home world settlers been here?" I asked.

"About five years ago," Turus said. "Everyone put down roots in the pretty places you flew over on your way here."

"Understandable."

"Part of the charter was to explore the rest of the planet and look for resources—minerals, fuel sources, precious gems and metals, and whatnot."

I nodded. It was the standard process taking place in lots of systems throughout the quadrant.

"When all of a sudden?" I said.

"We found this ancient city," Turus said. "There are other primitive ruins here and there over the planet. Collections of huts and old fire pits. But nothing like this."

As he said, a large complex of ruins came into view. It encompassed three towers flanked by a series of low, squat buildings assembled or carved from a dark gray material. Bright beacons shone from the tops of the towers. Flat-top pyramids sat between the larger structures. Craggy, yawning shapes like giant petrified trees stood around the edge of the complex. The sight of the sinister gray towers—one thousand feet in height each—gave me an ill feeling of familiarity. Turus watched for my response.

"What is it? You've seen something like this before?" he asked.

I was sure I had, but not in person.

""Let me ask the obvious question," I said. Why not just leave it be and move on? Let the scientists make sense of it."

"We would, but we've detected some special things about these towers," Turus said. "Especially the one in the center."

"What about the other two?" I asked.

"The other towers are quiet and empty," Dubbs said. "The main one is . . . not."

"Twelve men dead," Turus said.

"How did they die?"

"Well, our doctor was one of the dead, so we're just guessing now, but we think it's fear," Turus said.

"Something scared them to death?" I asked.

They glanced at me, looking for signs of skepticism. I believed them. I had seen many men and women frightened to death. It happens when dealing with the kinds of entities I encounter.

"You don't spook so easily, I hope," Turus said.

"I get spooked, yeah," I said. "It's a survival tactic. But I don't spook like the average person. I've seen too much."

Turus nodded. "Well, I guess that's bad for you, good for us."

"You said the temple wasn't empty?" I asked.

"You know all that good stuff I told you we were looking for?" Turus asked. "Our sensors have detected all of it in that tower. Precious metals. Enough power crystals to fuel fleets of ships throughout the galaxy. A real game changer. We can't let it go."

"Lots of money," I said.

"Yes, lots of money," Turus said, defensive. "And we'll give you plenty of it if you'll help us out."

"This planet has other resources you can use, right?" I asked.

"But the ones in these towers aren't naturally occurring," Turus said. "If our scans are accurate, there are stores of these materials. It's not like it's a mine or something. Besides, we have critical money and supply problems on the home world. What's in that tower will help a great deal, maybe even solve our worries with plenty left over. The consensus is that we're not going to let it all pass by on account of the tower being a damned haunted house."

"Despite twelve dead people?" I asked.

"*Because of* twelve dead people," Turus said. "We owe it to their memory to make this mission a success."

He turned back and stared at me hard. "So? You taking the job or am I turning around?"

"I'll take it."

He sped up.

The center tower loomed up high and wide as we got close. We arrived at base camp to find a somber mood among the workers.

"No one else will go into the tower, no matter how much we offer," Turus said. "Can't say I blame them. I won't either."

Workstations and tents sat thirty feet away from the tower's grand entrance. They had erected spotlights around the base to counter the heavy gloom. The sight of the majestic tower took my breath away. I could only speculate as to the bygone artistic genius who had designed it and the dedicated workers who had fashioned it. There was only the pale desert for miles. Where had all these materials come from?

Turus brought the hovercraft to a stop at the main tent. We all stepped off the vehicle. Turus announced my arrival to the gathered workers. They were eager to get back to work, but unsure what to make of me.

"Anything special you need?" Turus asked. "Did you bring your gizmos and ghost-hunting tools?"

I chuckled and tapped my temple. "My game is all played up here, Mr. Turus. Now, what specifics can you give me about the twelve men who died?"

"Not much," Turus said. "We sent them in. They died."

"Any video or audio recordings?"

"Sure, but all they show is men screaming out of the blue like scared children and dropping dead."

"Still, I'd like to see them."

They took me into the largest tent. Curtains of thick beige fabric divided the vast interior into smaller rooms. They led me along a curtained hallway and to a small room, where I received access to the last moments of all twelve men. They had worn bodycams that recorded their final moments. There wasn't much to see on the recordings other than darkness and gray walls. But the screams—they were among the worst I'd ever heard. In their dying moments, they tried to tell their fellow workers something. I jotted notes and replayed relevant footage to find out what they tried to say.

After I'd seen everything, I took a deep breath and consulted my notes. I had written phrases like *can't know* and *can't see here anymore* and *I can't know I won't know I don't want to know*, things of that nature. The common theme, best I could discern it, was they were being exposed to something—a visual or a piece of information—that they could not handle. Sentiments like *don't want to know* indicated a person of average knowledge confronted by horrible, unspeakable truths. Such exposure brought madness. Death followed soon after. This is why introduction to the forbidden is a cautious, gradual process.

And what of me? What hope did I have if confronted with the same phenomenon?

I thought about that. Suicide missions were not on my list at any price. However, as I had hinted to Mr. Turus, I had gazed into more than one abyss. Although insanity was a constant companion, forever

tapping me on the shoulder and inviting me to dance, it hadn't throt-
tled me yet. I had knowledge far beyond that of the average man or
woman. Whatever the entity in the tower had to frighten me with, I
hoped I would be ready. But my late father's voice echoed through my
memory, reminding me that no matter how much we think we've
learned, our understanding amounts to a speck in the boundless universe. The risk was as real to me as to the twelve unfortunates who had
gone before.

I had to consult the Library of the Ages. I stuck my head past the curtain that partitioned my room and asked to be undisturbed for a while.
Then I sat and cleared my mind. When I was calm and at rest, I
touched the white gemstone. After several minutes of quiet relaxation,
I opened my eyes into a timeworn library with scuffed wooden shelves
and tables piled high with dusty, cobwebbed books of various sizes.

So far, all I had to go on was the tower and the nature of the deaths.
Without the planet's correct name, and without knowing more about
the entity that lived in the tower, I was on little more than a fishing
expedition. However, towers of mystery and power were a recurring
motif in the strange histories and legends of the known worlds. It was
there I focused by energies. In the Library of the Ages, you can spend
hours in research only to open your eyes to reality and find you had
them closed for minutes. I read every tower reference I could find. My
memory would be my weapon when I entered this tower to confront
the entity. I did general research in advance, for I wouldn't dare access
the gateway in the presence of an otherworldly being.

Turus waited for me when I came out of the room.

"What do you think?" he asked.

"I agree with your original assessment," I said. "They were scared to
death."

"What could be so scary?"

"Based on their last words, they confronted sights, sounds, and
secrets that their minds could not comprehend. It scared the life out of
them."

He nodded. "So what does that mean for us?"

"It means we're most likely dealing with a powerful ancient entity," I said. "One who's been around for a very, *very* long time. And powerful. Such an entity is possibly a god, or in close association with a god."

"Can it be beaten?"

"It can. All beings are subject to powers given by the ultimate creator," I said. "We just have to figure out which tactics to use and have the courage to use them."

"Sounds like you have the plan," he said. "Can you put it into play and keep your sanity?"

"I'm going to try."

He chuckled. "That's not an answer."

"I can't say for sure, but I think I have an advantage."

"Oh? What advantage is that?"

I paused before leaving the tent. "I know how bad the darkness can get. I've seen it."

Everyone gathered behind me, thirty feet back among the safety of the small tent city they'd erected. It didn't escape my notice that a stretcher was close to hand should things go wrong. I stood at the base of the wide front steps of the tower. The dizzying vista was too much to take in at once. I looked side-to-side, looking for symbols or some clue as to the tower's purpose or origin. The facade was ornate and carved with horrible-looking beasts and humanoid creatures. Fluted columns and horizontal ridges rose into the clouds. But I saw nothing that gave it all a coherent meaning.

A single, rectangular stone box stood at the top of the stairs. It didn't belong. I pointed to the box and looked at Turus.

"What is that?"

He shrugged. "Looks like a coffin to me."

"No markings?"

"Illustrations and such. No words. As usual."

"Is it sealed?" I asked.

"Not sealed. Just a very heavy lid."

"Did you open it?"

"Thought about it. Based on what's been happening? We didn't dare."

I turned my attention back to the eternal majesty of the center tower. As I stood near the base, I couldn't escape the feeling that beings of enormous height had built it. I had to all but jump to get from step to step, and then each step took me four paces to cross. When I reached the top, I got a clear look at the portico as I caught my breath. The door stood open. Behind me, down at the base, all work had stopped. Everyone stood and watched.

I examined the stone sarcophagus. On its lid was a crude line drawing of a man with his hands around a long, upright pole. It was not familiar from any reading I had done.

I stepped closer to the door and spoke into the small radio they'd affixed to my ear. "How did you get the door open?"

"It was open when we got here," Turus's voice squawked in my ear receiver.

"Very well," I said. "You won't hear from me again until I come out."

If I come out was more accurate, but I needed as much optimism as I could muster.

I stepped through the portico and into the tower.

The presence of evil was right there, lurking just inside the entrance and hovering in the air throughout. Vaporous, rippled distortions skewed the view down the enormous main hallway and the side corridors, as if gas pipes had sprung a leak.

I worked to control my breathing. Whatever the previous twelve men felt in here, I felt it, too. Not enough to kill, but enough to weaken the resolve of anyone not used to such an atmosphere.

I pressed forward. Thick ridges lined the side walls. They stretched high and joined in a vaulted ceiling. I passed through the odd hallway as if walking through the ribcage of a giant dragon of the underworld. The smell of the place did nothing to dissuade me from that image. A dull, bleary red glow permeated the walls and floor, giving me just enough light to see around and above me.

A hissing sound came from the side walls. I expected it since I'd heard it on the doomed men's recordings. The hissing gave way to guttural growling that echoed in a hard and punishing way.

A horrible sensation flooded my brain. It took over my vision. I saw not the tower's interior, but terrifying, churning chaos. Screams, blood, fire. The vision that killed the others meant to invade my thoughts. As a means of defense, I imagined a thick, red velvet curtain. In my mind, the curtain fell and blocked the chaotic vision from view.

"I don't want to see it!" I yelled.

I hoped my voice sounded confident. The growling became more than just indiscriminate noise, and I froze in place. The entity was talking to me. I didn't understand or recognize the language.

"I can't understand you," I said. "If you are a majestic creature of the underworld. You understand all tongues."

"Cooorrrrect!" came the reply in that same awful voice. *"Youuuuu arrrre not liiiiike the otherrrrr onesssss."*

"Are you planning to kill me?"

"Oooooonly if you are of nooooo ussssssse to meeeee."

"I would prefer to live," I said.

"If you hellllp meeeee, you will beeeee rewarded!"

"Will helping you cause harm to others? To my soul? To the universe?"

I walked deeper into the hallway. As far as I could tell, I was further than any of the dead men had come. The soft red haze enveloped me, but I still couldn't see over ten feet ahead or behind. I turned back, but couldn't see the portico. The faint glow, it seemed, followed me. Now and then I sensed the air disturbed as if by great, fluttering wings. It came and went.

"Only the ignorant and obsceeeene are harrrrmed by knowinnng!"

As my eyes adjusted to the murky glow, I noticed a pattern on the walls. Crude line drawings. As I conversed with the voice, I drifted closer to the drawings to see if I recognized them.

The illustrations were of small creatures. Some were humanoid. Others animal-like. Most of them were creatures beyond human imagination. Above these was the image of a towering humanoid figure in a long, flowing black cloak. Black droplets fell from its hands and the hems of its robe. Its face was in shadow. There was no way to tell if the being was human or only resembled a human.

I pointed to the tall figure. "Is this you?"

"*Looooong ago.*"

It was difficult to control my breathing. I wanted nothing more than to run out of the tower in a panic. A revelation of something dark and horrible awaited. The heavy, oppressive fear gripped my chest and shook my hands and legs. As bad as the sensation was, it wasn't enough to kill a man, even a man unused to such a thickened, evil presence. There was more to come.

"I know something of the darker realms," I said, trying to sound confident. "You are a spirit. And if this image is you, that means you once had corporeal form. Which means someone defeated you."

A wave of nausea wracked my gut as the entity's fury thundered down the corridor like the smell of rotten meat.

"*Aaaaarrogant fooooool!*"

The sick feeling intensified. I felt death was near. A horrible, prolonged death induced by raving madness. I was at the brink of what killed the other twelve men. My mind's curtain undulated and swayed about, but I kept it closed.

Knowledge. That was my power. I had studied all known sects and groups, along with the beings and entities they worshiped. When not at a job like this, my duty was to spend time in the Library of the Ages, reading and learning, putting pieces together. I had only the faintest recognition of the icon on the wall, but there wasn't much to go on. Just a figure in black. The slave beings surrounding it were my best clue.

"Your soul is trapped here," I said.

Silence.

"Isn't it?"

Continued silence.

"You need help to be free, but so far no one has had the fortitude to withstand your presence."

Still, silence. But the sick feeling eased up a bit, although the rotting stench gusted through the corridor with greater power. I was glad I hadn't yet eaten that morning.

"But I know things," I said, stepping to the mural on the wall once again. "I am unique among men in my knowledge."

Velus was at the far reaches of the known universe, at least here in my day and time. As my ancestors spread out through space with their new technologies, the old ways carried with them. Some old explorers were sensitive to the words and thoughts of vast, horrible creatures who had fallen to extinction in days when planets still formed. The further into space they traveled, the more intense their "readings" of those voices became.

Those "sensitives" who heard these messages in their minds found each other and formed The Brotherhood of the Word. Soon they tasked themselves with writing down the communications from these unknown beings. If they heard of a madman raving in an asylum, the Brotherhood would go to him to write down his words. In their experience, there was no such thing as mindless ranting.

What the gathered knowledge of the Brotherhood revealed was so terrifying that the ruling councils of men decreed them forbidden and illegal. The Brotherhood went underground. They concealed their membership and mission with secret codes.

My father was a member of The Brotherhood. His position passed to me. I made daily study of the ancient texts, all written by hand. It was a life-preserving measure. In my profession, ignorance was lethal. Most of the knowledge was of unknown purpose or history. But you never knew when the unknown would become known. Then, it was best to be familiar with the words of those who received lost histories.

"For example," I said, trying to sound confident despite my fear. "These little beings here, with the appendages coming off their arms and legs. I've seen them before."

"Immmmposiblllle. I've never seeeeen your face beforrrre."

"My kind have powers, too. Powers of the mind and spirit. When you were defeated and raged at the stars, some of our kind were listening."

"Puny creaturrrres. Usefulll onnnnnly for their blooooooood!"

The next wave of terror was too much to bear. I put my hand on the disgusting, ridged wall for support. The entity's booming laughter wrenched my gut.

"But one of these puny ones got the better of you," I said, pushing my luck. "How?"

"Freeeee meeeee, and I willl bless you amoooong mennnn!"

"I should know who you are before I make such a bargain."

I regarded the strange humanoid creatures on the wall again, trying to match them with anything I'd seen in my studies. I longed to enter the ethereal library again, but doing it with this evil presence nearby would open the library and the Brotherhood to invasion. So, I searched my memory from my earlier researches. I filed through the information about mysterious towers. Soon, I found it. My eyes watered from the shock of the revelation. The entity picked up on my mood.

"You knooooow meeeee!"

There was no hiding it. "Yes, I do. You are Fidhumilati, High Priest of Galluch, the God of Madness."

A sinister wave of low-pitched guffaws roiled the corridor.

"Worship meeeeee!"

"There's only one way to kill a high priest of the old gods," I said. "I'm guessing the man in the sarcophagus outside was the one who did it. They placed him there to stand guard over you. To remind you of your defeat. Is that right?

"Liaaarrrrrrr!"

"Where was it done? Tell me the room where he did it."

"Freeeeee meeee heeeere!"

"And if you're freed? What then?"

Those in my line of work have to discern if an entity was more dangerous as a spirit or a corporeal being. It was often best to leave the spirits as they were, even if destructive. Let them have the building if necessary.

The spirit of High Priest Fidhumilati was slow to answer my question.

"Well? If I free you, what then?"

"Returrrrrn to aboooode!"

"What abode?"

"Lorrrrd of the worrrrrrld!"

"You wish to be lord of this planet?"

Just the thought of Fidhumilati turning the entire planet gray gave me an additional shudder.

"You're trapped here, aren't you?" I asked. "You fell victim to someone knowledgeable in the ancient texts. They caught you off-guard."

I walked to the mural again. The oppressive fear abated somewhat, as if Fidhumilati wanted to hear what I had to say. The black droplets under the black figure in the illustration caught my attention again. I had the answer.

"We're in the Shrine of the Possessing Rain, are we not?"

The weight of malevolent history fell upon my shoulders hard. A few people in my order knew of this infernal place, but few discussed it. There was considerable debate over whether the Temple existed or was mere legend. Sometimes, we had no way of making those distinctions. I had to get out as soon as possible.

"Freeeee meeeee and the tower shall beeeee yoursssss!"

"I don't want it," I said.

I tried to ease my way back toward the entrance, but there was no hiding my plans to escape.

"Freee meeee and live!"

"I'm aware of your history, even though I didn't realize this was the place. All of Velus used to look like this desert, didn't it? Because of you, everyone on this planet lived in the ashes of evil. Your insidious rain caused madness, and the inhabitants of this planet killed each other in their insane furies. But someone knew. A learned man or woman. Someone like me, privy to the secrets of the ancient gods. You were outwitted and beaten."

"Therrrre is much yooooou do not knooooow. Foooool!"

"I'm sure there is. But there are things I know. Your spirit is bound to this tower, is it not? Only a fool would dare release you to your body again."

Fidhumilati unleashed would bring destruction to the planet. If freed from the tower, he was still confined to this planet. His spirit could not carry through space. He dwelt in the inner realms of Velus. A spirit like him inhabited all planets. They called out until followers heard them and raised them up and unleashed evil upon their lands. In rare instances, as in Fidhumilati's case, a wiser human got the better of them.

No, Fidhumilati was best left as he was, blustering in his towering prison, content with frightening to death the occasional wayfarer who didn't turn back when he should.

"I'm leaving," I said.

"Youuuu willll not make it out aliiiiive!"

I wouldn't get paid, either. All terrible options, but doing anything else would go against everything I believed in, everything my ancestors and brethren in the field fought to preserve. Some spirits needed release. Some, like this one, needed eternal binding. I turned to go.

By the time I was halfway down the corridor, I thought I would escape. Someone interrupted me. Not Fidhumilati, as I feared, but by Turus and a squad of men bursting into the corridor.

"Stop there, Biringer," he said.

His men aimed their weapons at me. I didn't know why, but it soon made sense.

Turus had heard the entire conversation via my radio, of course. I should have shut if off, but I was unused to having such a device on me. Now he sensed what the spirit wanted in order to free up the tower for his plunder. Turus and his men were nervous but determined. No doubt he had convinced his men that the entity would not harm them if they were there to help it.

"I'm speaking to the spirit of this tower," Turus said.

A low growl rumbled through the corridor. The men shifted about and made sure their comrades are close.

"We will free you," Turus said. "If you spare us and give us the tower."

"You are fool, Turus!" I said. "The treasures you'll find here won't be worth the madness you'll receive."

"Quiet," he said.

"Centerrrrrr oooooof towerrrrrr!"

Everyone cowered, but stood their ground. Turus nodded and turned to his men. "Let's go! And bring him."

I got a rough escort to the center of the tower. The sick heaviness of fear stayed with me.

"You can let me go," I said. "This is your decision. Don't make me live with the consequences."

"We might need you," Turus said. "I'm sorry for the rude treatment. When this is over, you'll be paid double."

There was no reasoning with him. I would have to endure whatever lie ahead and hope to think myself out of any trouble.

The main corridor ended with a vast set of double doors carved with images transcendently evil in their beauty. Everyone gazed upon the door with awe. Then Turus shook his head, focused, and ordered the doors opened.

"Those images represent our fate if you continue," I said.

"I know that superstitions and legends are real, for the most part," Turus said. "I've been around enough to understand that. But you forget that technology is far more powerful and practical. And it is making inroads, as we are now. Be confident."

It took the entire company to pull the doors open. Everyone covered their noses at the awful stench of ancient death. The men lit up electric torches and the sweeping light revealed a wide chamber. The team backed out of the room when they saw what lie on the floor in the center.

It was the body of Fidhumilati. In life, he had been half a body length taller than the average man. The only visible flesh was his decayed hands and feet tipped with talons, and a long, oval-shaped face. The eye sockets were black. The remnants of the nose, reptilian. Sharp fangs lined a withered mouth. It yawned open in a scream of anguish and rage.

A pole made of an unknown black metal, about the thickness of a man's wrist, protruded from the high priest's chest.

Turus's men rebelled at the sight of the monstrous being. Turus shouted them down to argue that the beast was long dead, that I had the ritual that would get rid of its ghost, and untold riches awaited everyone. This calmed the brewing uprising, but everyone remained jittery. Turus turned to me, impatient and wanting me to take care of the nonsense before the men changed their minds.

"Well?" he asked. "Let's get on with it. Tell us what to do."

I sighed. There was no choice but to cooperate.

"You need to remove the pole," I said.

"That's it?" he asked. "You don't have to chant or wave a wand around?"

"The pole goes through his body and down past the crust of the planet."

He gave me a blank stare.

"That must be miles down," he said.

"Two miles, to be specific," Dubbs said.

Turus, still disbelieving, turned to look at the pole. Only three feet of it was visible.

"You're telling me this is the tip of a two mile long pole?" Turus asked.

"According to the ancient texts, a direct creation of the planet's elder god—which he was—had to be impaled by a pole long enough to reach into the mantle from which he spawned," I said. "He's pinned to his 'native soil,' so to speak."

"How in the world did they do that?"

"I don't know. The legends are short on details."

Turus nodded. "So we pull out the pole. What happens then?"

"Two things," I said. "Fidhumilati returns to life, and I'll be gone before I can see it happen."

"Sorry, Biringer," Turus said. "You're staying until we're sure this works and we have the tower."

I couldn't believe what I heard.

"Are you seeing this thing?" I asked, pointing to the body. "Think of how it makes you feel to look upon it when it's long dead. Now imagine how you'll feel when it's alive."

The men stirred, getting wobbly again. I waited for the voice of Fidhumilati to protest, but he remained silent. Perhaps necessary, now that we were in the inner sanctum. Turus glared at me.

"No more talk from you," he said. "When it's all over, you can go. Not a moment before. Don't make me have to bind and gag you."

"As you say," I said. "May I wait in the corridor? It's unnecessary for me to witness what will happen."

Turus nodded and gestured at two of his men to escort and guard me.

"If he tries to run, kill him."

The three of us left the chamber. My escorts seemed relieved.

Removing the pole was such a tedious chore that it muted the sinister nature of it all. It was so long they had to pull it up ten feet at a time. Then they cut it off and carried the fragment away. After that, they raised it another ten feet. This continued for two hours. The men took comfort in the mundane repetition of the task and relaxed. My guards joined the effort. They helped carry out pole fragments.

I considered making a run for my ship. I would have to steal a hovercraft, find my way back to the landing area, and hope my ship was unguarded. All unlikely. There was no choice but to wait and hope I survived.

By the end of the task, I had taken a seat on the floor of the main hall. A chorus of whoops sounded from the chamber. I knew that the final length of the pole had come free. Turus came out from the double doors.

"Biringer! Come in and see! We're done!"

Since I was a prisoner now rather than a hired hand, I decided I should at least satisfy my curiosity. I wondered at the moment what my father would think, what he would do.

I entered the chamber to find everyone staring at me. The body was still on the floor. It had not moved.

"Well?" Turus asked. "Is that it? Are we done here?"

"You've done all you can do," I said.

"That's not what I mean. Can we carry this thing out of here and get rid of it without a band of spooks coming down on our heads?"

"I don't know what will happen next," I said. "Fidhumilati is free from his binding. How he reacts to that? Only he knows. If you're asking me what I would do, then I'd say go ahead with your work."

"I can tell the air is different in here," Turus said. "How about you?"

I took a moment to get a sense of the atmosphere. He was right.

"Something's changed," I said. "The dark energy has left. The air is clean."

"That's good enough for me," Turus said.

He turned to his men.

"Okay, fellas, get this carcass out of here and get the exploratory teams ready to come in."

The men sprung into action. Turus walked up to me.

"Well, I guess you've completed the job," he said.

He took out a computer tablet and tapped in some commands.

"I've sent your payment," he said. "I'll radio for a hovercraft to take you back to your ship."

He shook my hand.

"Sorry about the rough stuff," he said.

"I've been through worse," I said. "Best of luck with your treasure hunt."

We parted. He returned to the chamber while I hurried out of the tower. I found a hovercraft with a soldier standing near it. He nodded at my approach. I was almost to the craft when screams came from inside the tower. My pilot looked at the tower in shock.

"We need to leave!" I said.

His radio squawked.

"Sorry, sir!"

He ran off with his rifle into the tower. All over the base camp, hundreds of men and women scurried into action. I cursed under my breath and hopped on the hovercraft. I hoped to commandeer the vehicle and leave on my own. The control panel was unfamiliar, but I hoped I could maneuver it just well enough to avoid killing myself or anyone else.

Men came running out of the tower. It was no surprise to see them all struggling with sudden onset insanity. They screamed and fought with each other like rabid animals.

So Fidhumilati, High Priest of Galluch the God of Madness, was reborn.

"You fools. You fools!"

It was all I could think to say. There was nowhere to run. I scrambled to get the hovercraft operational.

The towering figure stepped out of the tower in all his malevolent splendor. He looked around at the panicked chaos and laughed that familiar laugh. Soon his gaze settled on me. I figured death was upon me.

He lifted his head. He recognized me. His hood eased back, and I saw that his face had not changed from that of a centuries-old corpse. The only difference was his eyes. They were large white orbs. The irises were rimmed in yellow and centered in red. It was the most terrifying visage I had ever seen.

To my surprise, Fidhumilati looked away, as if already bored with me and our conversation.

He raised his long arms into the air and shouted an infernal incantation I was glad to not understand. His body, along with his cloak, bubbled like hot oil. In seconds, millions of black particles left the high priest's body and floated into the air. Now I knew why this beast had forgone a personal killing. He planned to use his special dark power to possess us and force us to kill ourselves with madness, just as he had infected those in the tower.

I had to get out from under the black rain about to fall. I ran my leg muscles to fatigue in my effort to get to the nearest tent. The other soldiers and crew still ran about in panic, firing their weapons in vain at the monster and watching dumbly when he transformed into an oily mist.

I had just gone under the tent's awning when the possessing rain fell. I watched, horrified, as the black downpour covered everyone else. At first, everyone reacted as if they expected an acidic, corrosive effect, but it was worse than that. Nearby, a man and a woman screamed in harsh terror. My eyes opened wide as the black substance entered their pores. In seconds, the pair screamed and thrashed in madness.

They set up on each other, punching, clawing, biting. I didn't dare intervene. I could not turn my eyes away from the massacre. Limbs were torn from bodies. Eyes pulled from their sockets. The gray sands were soaked red from the cannibalistic frenzy. On the giant steps I saw Turus, covered in blood. I refused to think about what he had done in his frenzied state. He scanned the steps and ran like a madman into chaos. Fidhumilati looked around, pleased at the destruction he had wrought. I could tell, even through his skeletal face, that not all was right.

There was a survivor. Fidhumilati was not pleased. Only one person had dodged the possessing rain. Me. The high priest looked around as he descended the steps. He spotted me huddled under the awning.

Black rain continued to patter down. The atmosphere of this wicked land responded to the dark cleric's commands and helped spread the foul downpour all across the gray desert.

The dark figure roared in fury. It was intimidating, but I also felt hope. If he could kill me, he would already have done so. As a spirit, the creature revealed the infernal secrets of the underworlds beyond and frightened his victims to death. As an incorporated being, he had the power of the black rain to enslave. I was too educated in the forbidden secrets to suffer lethal fear. I had outwitted his rain by taking shelter. For now, I was safe, but how long could I just sit under a tent? At any second, Fidhumilati would no doubt chase me down and force the rain down my throat. He was that large and powerful.

He never chased me down. Instead, he stood on the tower steps, watching me with contempt in his awful eyes.

"I haaaave an eterrrrrity to waaaait! Hoooow looong can youuuuuu wait?"

He had an eternity. I had about three days before dying of thirst. A scan of the complex showed the rain continuing without pause. There was no escape. My ship was too far to run. Even the short distance to the hovercraft would expose me to the rain. I refused to surrender to the dark being. If a slow death by thirst was the only way to escape, then so be it.

I touched the leather bracelet on my wrist. It was tempting to touch the gemstone and enter the library in search of answers. Still, I dared not do it. If Fidhumilati sensed the open gateway and entered through it . . . well, it was too much to contemplate.

The infected continued to attack each other. Their numbers dwindled. They left me alone as I hid. Their minds were too primal and addled to conduct a search. Soon the battle moved away from the shrine, as the poor possessed creatures ran off to continue their violent revel elsewhere.

By the third day of the standoff, my stomach growled. I ached of thirst. My mouth was dry and my head throbbed in pain. At the sight of me, weak and slouched on my knees, I thought I detected the faintest smile curl up on his awful face. I could forgo food for quite a while, but without water, I was near the end. He knew it.

Beyond the awning, the dark rain continued to fall. The oily black drops rose from the High Priest's body and fell. The drops crawled along the gray sand and returned to him, and the cycle repeated and kept me trapped. A bolt of pain wracked my gut. I doubled over. The dark one laughed at me without mercy.

"Soooooon youuuuu will dieeeee. Give innnn to your faaaate!"

I rose to my knees. It took most of my remaining energy. Death was near. I could let myself go. My soul would be safe from Fidhumilati, but that would only benefit me. Unless I found a way to defeat him, the dark priest would carry on his domination. What remained of the planet's beauty would become corrupted, gray, and filthy under his reign. There had to be an answer that escaped my thoughts.

I remembered how I resisted the fear in the tower corridor. Training against surrender to fear is a basic skill of our order. Resistance to fear is the greatest power and can open doors of possibility unknown even to the grand masters of the Brotherhood.

I stumbled forward. Twice I fell and had to struggle to my feet. Perhaps I had waited too long. My vision was blurry and spotty. I gathered whatever wits I had left and staggered out from under the safety of the awning. Fidhumilati cackled and clapped his hands together.

"Gooooood! Coooome to meeee! Embraaaace your maaaaassssssster!"

My arms shook as I lifted my hands to the air. The ugly black rain pelted my skin. I felt the unpleasant sensation of the substance entering my skin. I steeled myself. The rain invaded my body and attacked my sanity. I focused my thoughts on the bright light of the ultimate creator of our universe, the most benevolent Master of All.

I convulsed from weakness as the black rain worked hard to seize my exhausted mind. Despite my torture, I was winning. Fidhumilati growled, impatient. In his arrogance, he had no worry yet of defeat.

As the masters had foretold, my courageous act opened alternative possibilities,. An idea came to me. Since I didn't speak the language of this planet, and since their communication was visual, I put an image in my thoughts of what I intended. The assault on my mind faded. The high priest looked concerned.

"Whaaaat arrrre you saaaaaaying?"

An odd, distasteful surge of strength fortified my body. Black droplets flew from Fidhumilati's body and into mine. The high priest sensed something amiss and turned to retreat into the tower. He couldn't get away. His eyes widened with alarm. I was drawing his physical body into mine, drop by drop. I was the stronger one now.

Helpless, he thrashed and roared in fury and terror. As the last drops of him sailed toward my body, he let out a final, anguished scream of defeat, a scream that finished from my own mouth as I consumed him.

I stood triumphant. It was the wrong emotion, though. It was the influence of the dark priest. I had to take care of his essence right away, for I could not control his personality for much longer. He was much more powerful.

The path to expanding knowledge remained open to me. There was no way to know how long it would be so. I staggered up the tower stairs. My unbalanced gait was due not to my hunger and thirst, but from adjusting to the power of Fidhumilati slithering within me.

My strength gave way as I reached the top. I collapsed against the stone sarcophagus. Again I studied the image on the lid—a man holding a pole. I had it now. This was the grave of the one who had subdued Fidhumilati so long ago. His tomb had been placed here as a sentry against the monster, a mocking of its power, or both.

The entity's essence—at internal war with my own—fought against me. Proximity to the tomb brought out a surge of panic and power that overwhelmed me. I pushed it back.

The sarcophagus's lid was unsealed. It was heavy. It took me several minutes to push it away. There, inside, was a skeleton wearing the remnants of a rotted green robe. Its bony hands clutched a pole as long as the body.

There was little time left. I leaned over into the sarcophagus and forced the black substance out of my body. It escaped from my head through my eyes, ears, nose, and mouth. A most unpleasant experience. My eyes went black for a moment as I freed myself of the muck.

The black stuff poured into the tomb and there it stayed—trapped by the power of the ancient man which still lived in his grave. It was my victory over fear that allowed me to know this.

The last of the bilious glop dripped from my mouth. I exhaled with relief. My exultation at the win gave me enough strength to return the lid to the tomb. Fidhumilati was trapped again, only this time in a much smaller space.

I found a tent provisioned with food and water. That and a few minutes rest gave me the strength to steer the hovercraft back to my ship. The sad evidence of the widespread nature of Fidhumilati's attack was apparent everywhere. Mangled bodies lined the streets and outposts. Back at the courtyard, the landing zone was quiet.

My ship roared to life. I flew over the complex and past the towers. I wondered how long the essence of Fidhumilati would remain imprisoned. Nothing was permanent in our universe. The tower had much wealth to offer. Other men and women would come for it. Other entities from other planets would reach out into the minds of willing humans and call them to sinister worship. And the Brotherhood of the Word would stand ready to enter the void.

I left the skies of Velus and returned to the vastness of space. Space that—as any member of the Brotherhood could tell you—was anything but empty.

Douglas Walker's Appeal

My name is Douglas Walker. I am aware of my surroundings, my identity, and my existence. Despite what the world will be told about me, I am of sound mind. It is the world and its hidden circumstances that are insane. Not me. My most aching fear, out of many, is that I will not be believed. I am afraid I will be remembered as a madman. I am not mad. I made mistakes. I took notice of entities and dimensions that took reciprocal notice of me, but I kept my sanity. I cannot stand being thought insane. If expanding my mind to hidden truths is insanity, then lock my cell door forever. This statement will prove my rationality. I swear upon that which I and anyone else hold sacred that the following events happened as described.

It all began with an evening out with some chums of mine. Of my circle of friends, I am the most calm and reserved. The one who must be dragged to anything new and exotic. So it was that night. They brought me to a medium. Conversation with the dead seemed like a novel way to pass an evening, they reasoned. I rolled my eyes at the silly idea, but upon entering the medium's modest home, I was intrigued.

We stepped into another, exotic world. The smell of incense was intoxicating. Candles burned just bright enough to see and were spaced apart to keep the mood mysterious. Talismans and religious-looking objects lined the walls, shelves, and tables. Velvet tapestries decorated the walls. Some of them depicted scenes that made me blush.

The medium emerged from behind a beaded curtain. She was elegant and lithe. I was entranced. Her eyes were dark brown and gazed up at us from her slightly lowered head. This was meant to imply shyness, but we weren't fooled. We knew in an instant that great power lay behind those beautiful eyes.

She beckoned us to sit at a magnificent mahogany table. The four of us took our seats. My thrill at sitting next to her thankfully went unnoticed. With long, slender fingers she examined our palms. My friends each got fortunes I thought were mundane. It took energy out of the experience for me. When she took my hands, I was alert again. I tried not to jump at the tickling sensation of her small hands caressing mine. She traced her fingertip around the creases in my palm. Suddenly, she gave my hand a quick squeeze, as if she'd received a mild electric shock.

Her eyes darted up to mine and away again. Something had surprised or disturbed her. My companions watched us, frowning. She smiled again and put us in her thrall once more. My palm was difficult to read, she told me. Perhaps my future was cloudy. I accepted that, trusting those eyes and her soft voice.

She moved on to channeling spirits. It all seemed vague and uninteresting to me. Where did my deceased grandfather leave his pipe? Those were the questions my friends had. They got their answers. I had nothing to ask. She volunteered no information to me, gave no indication that an ancestor wanted to tell me about hidden treasure behind the paneling.

It was an entertaining enough way to spend an evening. The lady was pleasant to interact with and beautiful to see. One of my group paid her for her services, and each of us offered a generous tip. As we excused ourselves from the table to leave, she took gentle hold of my arm.

"There is more to you than you," she said. "You have on your hands the markings of an old race, a people who called Earth home before the pyramids of Egypt rose to the sky."

I was at a loss to respond.

"You have come among the spirits and sat where the veil is thin," she said. "Be careful."

I assured her I would be careful and thanked her for the warning. My companions stood in the doorway, watching us with curious looks. I shrugged as I approached them. They got specific details regarding this or that item from dead relatives. I got some fiddle-faddle about pre-Egyptian ancestors. At her front door, I paused and glanced back, nodding my thanks. She gave me a stiff smile and a wave. She looked worried. My friends and I closed the evening with a few pints of bitter. They discussed the experience. According to them, the lady had taken a special interest in me. They suggested I return the next day to invite her to dinner. When I thought of the medium, I remembered her beautiful face, delicate touch, and quirky surroundings. Her bizarre warnings were forgotten.

The following morning I rose from a restless sleep, not anxious to begin a new week at work with so little rest. I felt hollow and unrested, as if I were on the downside of a brief illness. A check of the clock showed I had overslept. That was strange. The alarm was set, but I must have shut it off in a sleepy daze and fallen back to sleep. My irritation grew when I swung my feet out from under the warmth of the coverings to the floor. My toes hit cold wood. My slippers were not sitting on the floor where I left them when I retired the night before. Just the sort of morning irritation you encounter sometimes. I reached for my robe, only to find another surprise when my hand grasped at air where my robe had hung on its hook just last night.

By now I was suspicious that a trespasser had played a prank, for I saw no reason for a thief to break into a house in order to make off with slippers and a robe. I struck a match and moved to light the bedside candle. I'm sure I don't have to tell you that the candle was not there.

Although there could have been an explanation for this strange start to my day, a sobering air of unease settled around me. My eyes had adjusted to the early morning darkness. I looked about the room and saw that nothing else appeared to be missing. I convinced myself I had misplaced my robe and slippers and stood to make my way to the bath.

The wood floor chilled my bare soles. The crisp morning air raised goosebumps on my naked arms. I stepped into the bathroom and into another strange circumstance. The candle I could not find earlier sat on the sink where I placed it while I cleaned in the morning. However, it was apparent the candle had burned for some time. It was a mere stub of what it had been last night. The wax had run down the sink and hardened on the floor. The pitiful flame flickered as if it knew it was about to burn itself out.

Just as I had registered this bizarre scene, I noticed I no longer felt cold. The air was warm and humid around me. A damp layer of fog covered the mirror. The only conclusion was that a warm bath had already been run. With no small amount of fear, I peered into the tub. My heart quickened at the sight of pooled water around the drain. I glanced at my feet. The bath mat had wet footprints soaked into it. I am not sure what compelled me to do what I did, but I placed my own bare foot into the damp footprint on the mat. A perfect match!

I felt a rush of relief. I was confident now that the entire odd episode was because of nothing more malevolent than a simple case of sleep-walking on my part. I chuckled at the thought I had bathed in my sleep! Before I could rest easy, that damned logic in my brain asked its questions.

I ran my fingers through my hair. It was not damp, nor did it feel freshly washed. My mouth still had that disagreeable aftertaste from the previous evening's pints. My body still carried a feeling of unclean-ness. I posed the ominous question to myself: Who had used my bath? I am a bachelor and live alone. No one has a key to my apartment, save for my elderly landlord, who isn't the type to pull mischief like this. I now feared an intruder.

I jogged back to my bed, opened a drawer, and unlocked a small lock-box. There I retrieved a pistol I kept for potential danger. I searched every room for the invader that had so rudely helped himself to my personals. The last room I checked was the small kitchenette which was also the entrance to my apartment. Verifying the kitchen was empty, I knew I was alone. I felt relief, but I could not ignore the growing sense of mystery as to what had happened while I slept. I put the pistol on the counter and saw another unexplainable sight.

A loaf of bread, only purchased yesterday, lay on the counter next to a bread knife. A quarter of the loaf was gone. A cube of butter sat next to the bread with several pats cut away. A pot of water sat on the stove. I touched it and found it warm. A nearby coffee mug was half-full. My gaze shifted from the counter to the front door. The two deadbolt locks were secure, but the sliding chain lock hung useless and unfastened. I distinctly remembered sliding that lock in place last night. As I am sure you know, New York City is not always a safe place. I realized with unease that the only lock undone was the one that locked from the inside.

I noticed the clock and realized the day was getting away. I must get dressed and make my way to the accounting office in time for work. I dashed back to the bedroom, only to find—to no great surprise, I'm afraid—that someone else had already rummaged through my clothing. The only items missing were the clothes I had laid out for myself last night. My suit, socks, shoes, and so on. I considered alerting the police, but decided against it until I could formulate an explanation on my own. I could not think of one law that had been broken. The officers might think me mad. I got dressed and went downstairs.

As I walked out into the brisk morning air, I reached into my vest pocket to check the time. Alas, I had forgotten that my pocket watch was also missing. I had noted the time before I left my apartment and decided I still had sufficient time to walk to work instead of taking the Hansom, as was my custom.

On the first street corner stood young Robert, shouting out for people to buy a newspaper. Robert had worked my corner for a year now. As I approached him, he spotted me and frowned. Usually, he greeted me with a smile. The optimistic attitude that greeted me with the fresh air vanished. The odd, dreadful feeling from this morning returned.

Trying to ignore my trepidation, I greeted the young man with a smile and held out a handful of coins for the paper. His response startled me.

"Another paper, sir?"

I asked the young man what he meant by his unusual question. I feared I knew the answer.

"You bought a paper not a half-hour ago, sir."

His words were arrows of fear. I struggled to maintain my composure. I played the situation as if I were pulling a joke. I hoped this method would elicit answers. I chuckled and asked him if he was sure it was me.

"Of course, sir. You were on your way to the Greenlaw Accounting Office, just like you do every morning. You were in a terrible mood then, sir. Are you all right now? Have you lost the first paper?"

I tried to reckon what the lad meant by "terrible mood" as I strained to plan an answer to his question. I told him that, yes, I had indeed lost my first paper.

"Would you care for another, sir? I won't charge you."

The young man's generosity moved me. I couldn't avail myself of a free newspaper at a young boy's expense. I told the youth that it was my mistake. I paid for a replacement.

Now there was more added tension. Not only was there an impostor going through my daily routine in my place, but based on the newsie's reaction, this impostor looked just like me. A twin. Now I had a second witness to the strange impersonator, but I still had no clue who he was or what his motives were. I quickened my pace, determined to reach my place of work and confront my tormentor, for it seemed a natural assumption I would find him there.

I approached my employer's building and found a chaotic scene. Several police officers milled about the entrance. I was struck by an oppressive air of foreboding, worse than any before. Although I tried hard to ignore the sensation, I could not escape the nagging conviction that whatever the police had gathered for likely involved my double.

Call it intuition or instinct, but I shrank back among the growing crowd of curious onlookers. I spotted my coworker, Howard. He was one of my companions from the night before. We worked together. I angled my way toward him and tapped him on the shoulder. When he turned to face me, his face turned white.

"Douglas!" He looked around in apprehension. His voice was a fearful whisper. "What on Earth are you doing here?"

I dumbly informed Howard that I worked there.

He took my arm and led me away to an alcove and shielded me from view with his body. "Are you mad? They are all here looking for you!"

I knew they were not looking for *me*, specifically, but I still did not have any solid proof of my situation. I asked Howard what had happened. I did not think it possible, but he grew even more pale.

"Andrew Greenlaw is dead."

I put it together right away. My doppelgänger had murdered my employer. Because he looked just like me, I would be suspected as well as him. In his cunning, would he hide away until I took the blame for the crime? Or was he a madman, rushing around with blood on his hands and not a care in the world? I asked how the murder had been committed.

"The police aren't talking, of course," Howard told me. "The rumor is that the murderer used his bare hands. It's a dreadful sight, they say."

I asked him why they suspected me.

"Several people claim to have seen you leave by the front entrance covered in blood."

I thought about pointing out that I stood before him clean of any blood. But such an alibi could be explained away by a clever prosecutor. Either way, I knew my double was a murdering beast. Where had he gone?

I stood silent as a new feeling grew within me: bewilderment. What a morning it had been. Confusion, anger, fear and now a feeling of total indecision. I considered—but quashed—the idea of giving myself in to the authorities. The idea that my innocence could withstand any challenge, even from the Netherworld, seemed very naïve.

"Douglas."

Howard's voice brought me back from my rumination.

"Douglas, are you all right?"

He tried to hide the tone in his voice that suggested he was trying to evaluate my sanity, but I detected it. I told him I was fine under the circumstances, and that while I could not explain what had happened, I did not kill Andrew Greenlaw.

"Very well, then. You must leave and hide until the actual murderer is found. The crowd is focused on the events within the building, but it is only a matter of time before someone recognizes you. Forgive me, Douglas, but if I'm asked, I must deny we've had this conversation."

I understood.

"Good luck, my friend," he said.

Without a word, I slipped away through the curiosity seekers, expecting at any minute for a man to point or a woman to shriek and expose me. Andrew Greenlaw was a well-loved businessman and philanthropist in the neighborhood. The crowd's grumblings grew increasingly angry. Thinking fate might finally maneuver in my favor, I made it unmolested down the block, crossed the street, and entered the park. There I found a bench to sit and gather my thoughts. I had no hat to hide under. My infernal twin had taken it, of course. I could see the Greenlaw Building at the end of the street. The pack grew larger. My apprehension grew so intense that I felt ill. A strange voice startled me.

"Excuse me, sir, do you need help?"

I was visibly startled by the sight and sound of a policeman. I cursed myself, for surely my frightened reaction did nothing but enhance any suspicion he had. I nodded and—in a voice that was far too high--pitched for my comfort—assured him that everything was fine.

"May I have your name please?"

I had not prepared for such questioning. I stuttered under the glare of the officer, who was quite large and stern-looking. I tossed off an artificial name which he disbelieved.

"Sir, stand up, please."

I remained seated and looked around, trying to think of what to say to assuage his skepticism. As the officer laid his large hand on my shoulder, there arose a commotion from the corner of the block that housed the Greenlaw Building. A man rounded the corner in a frantic run. He shouted something that I could not hear at first. The assembled crowd turned in almost comical unison to see what he was doing. As he got closer, several officers emerged from the throng to confront him. Not sure whether this was the murderer they were seeking, they ordered him to stop. He stopped but continued to shout. I could now hear what he was saying.

"He's entered the warehouse! The murdering fiend has entered the warehouse around the block! I swear I saw the blood on his hands!"

The officers, now fearing a lynch mob, ordered the man to be silent. It was too late. The crowd shouted about their right to lynch a madman. A solid grip on my shoulder reminded me of my immediate predicament.

"Sir, I am asking you to come with me."

He all but lifted me to my feet. He meant to escort me to the Greenlaw building for interrogation by the officers there. I knew that once he took me across the street, I was doomed for sure, either by vigilante wrath or by police hell-bent on a quick resolution to their case. Was I to trust in reason? To point out that my clothes were clean and my hands free of blood? What kind of killer does the deed, runs home to wash and change, then returns to the scene of the crime to present himself for arrest? I had little faith that reason would overcome the madness of the mob.

The crowd, having heard the man scream the location of the suspect's escape, moved in that direction, ignoring the orders and pleas of the officers to stay still. Their loud and angry shouts, coupled with a dissonant chorus of police whistles, made for a chaotic symphony. My escort continued to steer me in that direction. We were on a near collision course with the mob. Soon we were close enough to hear the individual shouts and threats being uttered. I turned to plead with my captor to route us in another direction, when suddenly, just as I had feared, someone recognized me!

"There's the monster!" I heard a man shout as he pointed at me.

"It's Douglas Walker! He's returned to admire his bloody handiwork!" shouted another.

I struggled against the officer's grip. The officer, hearing the man's shout, hardened his suspicions toward me. He enveloped me in a powerful hug. The crowd shifted their attention away from the warehouse and bore down on me and my captor. My arresting officer ordered them to stay back. They did not listen. They intended to avenge Greenlaw's death by throwing on the same bloody robe of murder they accused me of wearing.

Through the chaos, I noticed several people standing at the distant edge of the mob looking toward the warehouse. They frowned and talked urgently among themselves, still curious about the sighting of a bloody suspect running into the building. There was still enough doubt in the air that it might save me. I realized that finding the true killer was my only hope if I meant to prove my innocence.

I relaxed my body and ceased struggling against the officer's grip. My actions fooled the officer into thinking I had given up. He eased his hold on me. The moment he did so, I broke free and ran toward the warehouse.

The crowd erupted in shouts of rage. The group of furious men and women reacted as a dog spotting a fleeing rabbit. They chased me, but my youthful legs and adrenalized fear gave me the advantage. I looked behind me as I ran and saw citizens shouting for my blood and officers shouting for me to stop.

I reached the door with the pursuing mob only a quarter length of the block behind me. I rattled the doorknob in desperation, but found it locked. The crowd grew louder. I feared violent hands on me at any moment. I sized up the frosted glass door and made my decision. I stepped back, tucked in my shoulder, and smashed through the door. The jagged shards tore at my flesh. Soon I would be just as bloody as

Greenlaw's murderer.

The warehouse was vast and complex. A man could hide for days in this massive building if he were clever enough. I thanked whatever gods might be watching when I spotted the security bar resting near the entrance. I clutched the heavy bar and slid it into the metal hooks fastened to the wall on either side of the front doors. Seconds after I did this, the mob reached the entrance. They could have crawled under the bar, but in their homicidal rage they fought and jostled with each other, making it impossible for anyone to come in until they made a more coordinated effort.

I jogged away, out of sight of the front entrance. I looked around, wondering where my double might have gone. Then an odd thought struck me: Where could I go?

As I ran deeper into the building, I pondered the answer to that question. If the intruder were indeed some sinister duplicate of myself, I had insight into its thinking. A stairwell led upstairs, but I passed it by. It was the first option to escape and seemed too obvious.

I turned down a hall and found the employee ' restrooms. I dashed into the ladies' room, reasoning that the men—despite being out of their rational minds—would avoid that area. And if a group of women went in there to investigate, I could fight them off more easily rather than a group of men.

In a far stall, I sat on a toilet with my feet up, feeling like an utter fool. Several minutes passed, and no one entered. I heard distant shouts and footsteps clanging on metal stairs. They were scouring the upstairs and downstairs sections.

I knew I could not stay there forever. The warehouse would bustle with the morning shift gearing up for another day's work. The police would soon seal all exits from the building, and here I sat. The voices grew more distant. It wasn't long before my impatience got the better of me. I crept toward the door, eased it forward, and peered out.

The crowd had grown weary from the chase, and their minds had cooled. From the small opening, I spotted several officers directing people. That the police had restored order only saved me from lynching, not arrest. They could commence their own search for the killer in minutes. I overheard the conversation of a nearby officer and his subordinate.

"Someone saw him go upstairs. I want you to take three men and go join the others already up there."

The officer scampered off to obey. I looked upon the ranking officer with some measure of curiosity. His uniform looked big enough for a man twice his size, and the cap rested precariously on his ears. I cannot tell you my utter horror when the man turned to face me! My fear multiplied to unthinkable proportions when I saw the man's face and realized I could have been looking into a mirror. I had stumbled upon my impersonator!

The fiend registered a similar look of astonishment. I feared his attack, but was surprised when he ran away. I considered an escape attempt to leave my double to be found by lawmen. However, the police now controlled the building. Any exit was certainly guarded. Capturing this strange intruder was my only hope of proving my innocence. I was sick with fear, but I steeled myself to the task at hand and gave chase.

I burst from the restroom just in time to see my prey round a corner and descend a stairwell. The policeman's cap fell from his head. I sadly wondered what had become of the rightful owner of his stolen uniform. The thing paused when I reached the top of the stairs and looked back at me. Emboldened by the look of fear in his eyes, I ran harder as the murderer went down, where I knew there was no escape—for either of us.

At the bottom step, I was swallowed by heavy darkness. A door boomed shut in the distance. I felt my way along the wall, trying to move toward the sound. My hands fell upon a heavy metal door. I reached for a doorknob and found none. Instead, I pushed the door and felt a rush of relief when it gave way.

A strange glow emerged from the room. It looked like moonlight, but I stood in a windowless basement and the sun had risen. The room had no furnishings. The floor was little more than packed dirt. I wondered what use any company had for such a room.

A hall led off to the left at the far end. I couldn't see its destination from my vantage point, but I could tell the light emerged from a source along that hallway. I stepped forward, bracing myself for my impersonator to leap at me from around the corner. He was not there, but yet another odd sight greeted me on this strangest of days.

A stone staircase, ancient in appearance, wound down before me and out of sight. I could only suspect that the company that ran this warehouse used it for storage. I paused at the edge of the stairs and turned to look behind me. I felt I had no choice. At any moment, the police would discover this path and follow. Most likely, they had found their fallen comrade, who provided the murderer with his disguise. So far as they knew, I was the beast they were hunting. They would show no mercy when they found me, especially in the secluded depths of this building. Once again, my only hope to survive this bizarre situation was to apprehend the murderer myself. I could confront my mysterious enemy or face certain death at the hands of the police.

I took the stairs as fast as I could: two, even three steps at a time. The stone staircase wound in a tight spiral, however, and I found it difficult to descend with enough speed.

After a few minutes that seemed like thirty, I caught my breath and wondered how deep it went. Angry voices shouted overhead. I knew my escape route had been discovered. I resumed my flight down, feeling a chill as I plunged deeper and deeper into the Earth. Finally, I burst into a clearing at the base. The large clearing glowed in a strange silver light provided by torches fixed to the walls. Why the torches gave off silver light instead of orange, I never knew.

What follows will seem like the ravings of a lunatic mind. I swear upon the Virgin they are true. At first I rejoiced when I saw a ravaged body sprawled on the floor. The body was clad in the officer's uniform. A gruesome red hole yawned from its torso. I thought my foul impersonator had fallen over the stairs to his death. I realized that even the worst tumble could not create such a bizarre wound. Movement at the far end of this subterranean chamber chilled my enthusiasm and speculation. I do not know how to describe the creature that stood a short distance away from me. However, I shall try.

It stood half the height of a normal man. It was naked, yet it was not of human appearance beyond its head, arms and legs. It had no hair. Its sickly pink skin stretched over wiry limbs. A reptilian tail swished back and forth. The awful thing turned to look at me with bulging yellow eyes full of pure evil and hatred. It hissed at me through sharp teeth. Its clawed hands tugged at a loose stone in the wall. I stayed calm enough mind to realize the thing was trying to escape! I glanced at my duplicate and the ragged hole in its body where this thing had crawled out. Whatever had caused my duplicate to appear, it had been animated by this demon, who now had no use for my extra body. Footsteps, accompanied by shouts, pummeled down the stairs. If I could only restrain this evil beast until the police arrived, they would have no choice but to accept my innocence, despite the incredible scene.

I dashed at the creature with a newfound courage. The little imp tried to duck away, but my reflexes were sharp. Once I wrapped my arms around its cold midsection, it could not escape. It hissed and screeched in an awful voice. Long claws flailed at me, cutting me along my hands and forearms. The ruckus on the stairs grew louder and closer. Only for another moment did I need endure.

To my great relief, three policemen burst into the ancient chamber. Their shouts of anger turned to gasps of disbelief. They froze, dumbstruck at the sight of me struggling with the unearthly creature. I waited for them to come to my aid. They just stood there. I shouted out to them to help me, that this was the thing responsible for the crimes committed that day. One officer raised his pistol. Before I could admonish him to take careful aim, he fired. The bullet missed the creature but struck me in the hip like a blow from a hammer. The sudden pain forced me to release my grip on the monster, which then charged the officers. This time all three men raised their pistols and fired. The creature may have been from regions unknown, but it was just as susceptible to bullets as you or I. It fell to the ground without another sound.

For a moment, the room was silent except for our labored breathing. I clutched my wound, breathing hard and sweating. The policemen emptied their weapons of the spent shells and reloaded. As they did, the wall containing the loose stone shook. First one stone tumbled out of the opening and onto the floor, then another. Each successive falling stone exposed a greater horror. I crawled out of the way as the stones collapsed to reveal a terrifying wall of familiar yellow orbs. Soon the entire wall yawned open, and a wave of those dreadful monsters flooded the room. The officers shrieked in desperate horror as the creatures overwhelmed them. One creature approached me. I waited for my death. However, instead of sending me off with a vicious attack, the thing examined me for a moment. After a few seconds, it stood upright and joined the other monsters. They dispatched the officers in a manner I will not and cannot describe.

The hideous things attacked those men past the point of it being obvious they no longer lived. When the massacre was over, the creatures assumed an inexplicably calm demeanor. They gathered up their dead fellow and made their way back through the hole. The final ones to cross over picked up fallen stones and replaced them until the wall was intact once again. My double, no longer animated by the demon, had lost its resemblance to me. It looked more like a store mannequin.

I felt light in the head. My hip wound was serious, but not fatal. A greater problem was getting anyone to believe the true story. The demon was gone, as was my double. I was the only suspect in the deaths of Andrew Greenlaw and the officers before me. Running or even walking was out of the question. All I could do was wait for the next wave of officers to come. When they arrived, they stopped when they saw aftermath of the hellish battle. One of them spoke and demanded I explain myself.

I told the truth. The only thing supporting my story was the spectacular assault on the dead officers. Did they believe I had done that? It was the work of a beast, not a man. They seemed uncertain, but there was not a chance they would entertain my story for long. They looked at me with pity. I collapsed to the floor on my back.

I was mad. That is how I would be dealt with, I knew. I said nothing when they resumed their interrogation. In minutes I blacked out, only to awaken here, in this bed, inside what I assume is an asylum. The police have told me they searched for the medium to verify my story, but the address I gave them is empty. They examined the wall in the strange cellar and found it sturdy. The body of my doppelgänger was no longer my twin. They couldn't establish who it was. At least they considered my story.

The ferocity of the crimes and the strangeness of my defense will see me live out the rest of my days in this asylum. So be it. For posterity's sake, I hereby declare that I have never shed the blood of a living thing so long as I have lived. I am innocent of the crime they wish to accuse me of, so help me, God.

Note:

This testimony is entered into the case file of Douglas Walker, chief suspect in the murder spree of March 19, 1899, that took the lives of Andrew Greenlaw, four police officers named in the report and a fifth victim who remains unidentified. Witnesses at the Greenlaw Accounting Office verified Walker's identity as the murderer. It is noted for the record that eyewitness testimony was not in agreement on this matter. Some witnesses, including a police officer, swore that Mr. Walker was in a different location when the killer was seen fleeing the scene of the crime. These discrepancies are superseded by the fact of overwhelming direct and circumstantial evidence. Mr. Walker was examined by mental health professionals and judged insane. He was committed to Whitecrest Asylum for an indefinite period. This case is declared closed.

Capt. William Loor, New York City Police, March 25, 1899.

The Rainbow Temple

Eight days had passed since the *Karon* had put out from San Diego. It had been a treacherous voyage. Only Captain Wick's calm experience guided the vessel through endless storms, winds, and high waves. His crew had grown restless and grouchy. His passengers—who had chartered the vessel and hired him—put on a brave face, but he knew they questioned the wisdom of hiring him. Captain Wick himself grew weary of the relentless bad weather and wondered if his crew were right when they grumbled that God himself—or a more sinister personality —sought to warn them away from their destination. Only the man funding the voyage—Dr. Faber, a jovial, middle-aged man—kept a good-humored demeanor.

Their destination was another cause of unrest aboard the ship. No one had ever been to the island of Doroa, nor had they heard of it. Only Dr. Faber knew of it. He had approached Wick with an ancient map in hand. Faber beguiled the captain with tales of a lost island hiding treasure beyond imagination. Wick wasn't the kind of man to fall for the allure of riches and the romance of discovery, but the money Faber offered was enough to overcome any misgivings. If they found the treasure, everyone got a percentage. Wick was desperate to retire and willing to take chances if the pay was good. Their official mission was to collect sea water samples, should they be stopped and questioned.

The journey seemed like a bad idea until lookouts spotted the island on the eighth day. Wick and his first mate consulted their nautical maps. Dr. Faber stood by with a satisfied smile on his face.

"Well, Captain?" Faber asked. "Is that island on your maps?"

Wick looked up with a grin. "No. It isn't."

Excitement rippled through the bridge. The unknown island existed. And if Faber was right about the island, odds were good he was right about the treasure.

A landing party was assembled. Wick took four sturdy young men from his crew to offer any needed muscle and security. Wick rarely left the ship, but his first mate was experienced and trustworthy. This was the chance of a lifetime.

They were escorting Dr. Faber and his team of three. There was Bryer Contois, a spectacled, thin young man, still in college, who would need looking after in dangerous terrain. Maddix Williamson was large and athletic for an academic. He and Wick got along well. Both liked their whiskey and to arm-wrestle. Williamson could take care of himself.

The third member of Faber's party was Nilah Thomassen. She was a statuesque blonde whose presence and visage the crew admired. She was partners with Maddix. Wick was told the two were well known in their field for excavating lost ruins. He learned through drinking sessions and card games with Maddix that Faber had also paid them well for an unconventional assignment. Nilah was romantically attached to Maddix, so everyone knew to show respect.

It had been a long, trying voyage. When the landing party came ashore, it lightened their mood. The excitement and possibility of the unknown gave them renewed energy. They shouldered their packs and prepared to venture into the strange jungle. For a moment, they stood in the sand and looked at the dark, forbidding trees before them. Wick frowned.

"What kind of trees are those?" he asked.

Faber looked to Maddix and Nilah. They shrugged. No one had ever seen their kind.

The tree line started twenty feet from the water. The trunks were thin, three feet in circumference. An odd, feathery black bark covered them. A bizarre, organic oval-shaped growth topped the trees. Each growth was roughly the size of Wick's ship.

"I was expecting palm trees," said Jovan, one of the sailors.

"This is an amazing discovery," Nilah said.

She took out her camera and documented the strange vista.

"Is it safe to move in?" Wick asked.

He warily eyed the dark forest.

Faber looked to Maddix.

"The only way to know is to go in," Maddix said.

He and Nilah started forward. The others exchanged looks.

"We've come this far," Faber said. "I want to see the treasure."

He looked at Wick and his men.

"Don't you?"

Faber followed Maddix and Nilah. The sailors followed.

The temperature dropped ten degrees within minutes of entering the forest. After another few minutes, the temperature dropped again, and the humidity eased.

"This is the first time I haven't been covered in sweat in a week," Nilah said.

"The ground is sandy," Bryer said. "Hardly any undergrowth."

Wick unslung his rifle and held it ready. His men did the same. As a gesture of trust, he had armed Faber's team with revolvers. Bryer had required a few lessons. He was a smart kid and learned fast.

The further into the forest they went, the darker it became. Soon their eyes had to adjust to the shadows as if it were late evening.

"You know where we're going, Doc?" Maddix asked Faber.

Faber opened his map. It was a laminated copy of the original. Wick came up next to him and aimed his flashlight at the map.

"We're heading to the dead center of the island," Faber said.

"Still amazes me how perfectly round the island is," Wick said.

"Lots of perfectly round things in nature, Wick," Maddix said. "I wouldn't let it worry you."

Wick nodded. "Yeah, but I'm a cautious fellow."

He took out his compass and studied it. "Let's bear right. Heading to the center of a circle shouldn't be hard."

Finding the direction was easy, navigating the endless tree stumps was a challenge. Wick had to keep checking their position as the trees forced them off course. After three hours, he called for a rest break. Elroy, another one of his men, lit a lantern and the party gathered around it.

Rohon and Parlan, the remaining two sailors Wick had brought along, sat next to each other and gazed up at the treetops as they drank from their canteens.

"Look at that," Rohon said to the others.

He pointed up. They looked.

"The trees have more than one trunk," Rohon said.

Wick and Maddix shone their flashlights up to the treetops. Bryer stood, as if an additional three feet would give him a better view.

"Wow. Some of them have six or even eight trunks coming down," Bryer said. "Maybe we should get some wood and bark samples."

"Later," Maddix said. "Let's find our lost city of treasure first."

Nilah glanced at him and grinned. "All in on the fantasy, are we, Doctor Williamson?"

"Can't hurt to take a look," Maddix said.

He gave her a kiss.

"It'll be there," Faber said. "You'll see."

"Anything you'd care to tell us, Doc?" Rohon asked. "I can tell when people are holding back, and you're holding back."

"Oh, there might be some additional details," Faber said. "But I won't bore you with it until we find what we're looking for."

"We've got time," Rohon said. "Bore us."

Faber smiled. "When we get there."

Rohon was unsatisfied, but didn't push further.

Wick stood. "It's best we press on. If there are ruins ahead, they can give us shelter. It's late afternoon and we still don't know what lives in this jungle."

"Mood killer, Skipper," Jovan said.

"Fine, let's go find some topless mermaids, men," Wick said.

His men cheered.

"Begging your pardon, ma'am," Wick said to Nilah.

"Don't worry about it," she said. "I wouldn't mind seeing some mermaids myself."

Boredom set in as the expedition continued. Maddix trudged forward until he was next to Wick, who led the party.

"What do you think?" Maddix asked.

"I'm not much of an explorer," Wick said. "The sea is my domain. But this jungle. It's very quiet. I thought jungles were loud."

"I agree. That's a little strange," Maddix said. "Although, we're in an undiscovered land. We're the strange ones."

"That's not comforting."

"Sorry. How long until we reach the center, do you think?"

"Another couple of hours," Wick said. "I find myself excited and worried at the same time."

"I know what you mean. If we don't find treasure, we'll have to content ourselves with finding an undiscovered island."

"That's no compensation at all," Wick said.

"You'll be famous," Maddix said. "Interviews. Big book deals. Sort of like finding treasure, in its own right."

Wick thought about that. "That's better."

The captain called another break a few hours later.

"It's early evening," he said to the group as they sat and stretched. "I estimate we have two hours of sun left. If we don't find the city of treasure by then, we'll make camp. So, when we journey on, everyone keep an eye out for a good campsite, just in case."

Bryer paced around, anxious. His endurance amused Wick.

"Have a seat, Bryer," Wick said. "Eat. Save your strength."

The young man kept pacing. "These trees are incredible to me. I'd really like to know more."

"We could cut one down," Elroy said. "You'll have to haul it back to the beach, though."

Everyone laughed but Bryer.

"No cutting down trees," Nilah said. "We're not here to spoil anything."

"I'm not talking about cutting down trees," Bryer said. "Let's just take a sample. That won't kill a tree."

Nilah shrugged. "I suppose a sample wouldn't hurt. Might be the only thing we have to show."

"Do we really have time for this?" Faber asked.

Everyone looked to Wick, who checked his watch.

"You've got five minutes, kid," he said to Bryer.

Bryer studied a nearby trunk. He asked for Jovan's machete. He took the blade and swung it into the trunk. After wrestling the blade free, a thick maroon liquid oozed from the gash. Everyone stood to see and trained their lights on it.

"What is that?" Parlan asked.

"Some kind of sap?" Elroy said.

Jovan reached for it.

"Don't touch it," Maddix said. "We have no idea what it is or what effect it might have on our skin."

Nilah reached into her pack. "I have some empty jars. I'll collect some of it."

"Maybe we can make a new pancake syrup out of it," Jovan said.

"Way to keep your brain moving," Rohon said.

Nilah took the machete from Bryer and put the tip into the oozing fluid. Then she let a few drops fall into the specimen jar.

"Impressive," Maddix said. "You didn't spill."

"I'm a pro," she said.

"Okay, if you scientists are happy, I think we should get a move on," Faber said. "We're close, aren't we, Captain?"

"If your map is accurate," Wick said. "I think so."

When the dream came true, it wasn't as any of them had expected. First there was a rainbow beam of light on the sand. It cut through the darkness like the sun coming out from behind black clouds. The party stopped short at the sight of it. Slowly they continued. A second splash of color appeared. Then ten more. Then dozens, hundreds. Everywhere the trees were lit up with prismatic beams of color. It was dazzling and breathtaking, as if they had walked into a starfield of brilliant color.

Hearts pounded as they walked further into the phenomenon.

"It's like the sun shining on a giant diamond!" Rohon said.

"My boy," Faber said. "That's exactly what is happening."

They came to a vast clearing in the trees. Before them stood a colossal temple complex. There was a courtyard, a pyramidal temple with a staircase leading to the apex. There was a long, squat building with rooms like barracks. The entire collection of lost structures took some adjusting for their eyes.

The full complex was made of diamonds. Brilliant rainbow waves reflected everywhere. It was almost blinding.

Maddix led the way. He stepped off the sand and onto the diamond floor of the complex. The floor had a slight serration that gave traction for their boots. The rest of the team followed. They grinned madly at each other. Shards of refracted rainbow light covered everyone. They held up their hands and watched the color move over their bodies like tiny fairies. A wonderful gust of cool air swept across the open area.

"This is a dream!" Elroy said.

"I can't even process all that this means!" Bryer said.

Jovan pumped his fists in the air and roared in triumph. His outburst set off the others, and for several minutes everyone hooted and hollered and celebrated the amazing find. Wick grinned as he looked around in awe, but he was more subdued.

"This is the treasure then?" he asked Faber.

Everyone laughed at the dumb question as they settled down. Faber leaned in close to a section of the diamond wall, opened his mouth, and exhaled. A small patch of fog covered the diamond. It dissipated at once. Faber grinned. He took a jeweler's loupe from his pocket, held it to his eye, and examined the jeweled wall.

"Small imperfections," he said.

"Is that bad?" Rohon asked.

"No, it's good," Faber said.

The doctor snapped open a lighter and held the flame to an angled section of the diamond. After a few seconds, he took the lighter away and felt the surface with the back of his hand.

"The heat faded immediately," he said, looking up at the others with a giddy smile. "Diamonds are great heat conductors."

"Well?" Wick asked. "Real diamonds?"

Faber regarded the diamond wall. "Such brilliance and glitter. Yes, this is the treasure. There might be more conventional jewels and coins and what-not, but this is what we've come to find!"

Everyone cheered. The idea of riches was thrilling enough, but the beauty of an entire complex made of huge diamonds was hard to comprehend, even as they stood in the midst of it. All except for Wick.

"And how are we to benefit from this?" he asked. "Do you have a plan to raise a diamond city from the sand and sail back to the United States? Or shall we build homes here and sell tickets?"

"You really are a mood killer, skipper," Jovan said.

"He's right," Elroy said. "How does this make us rich?"

Wick and his men formed a menacing half-circle around Dr. Faber. Maddix stepped forward.

"Easy, fellas," Maddix said.

"Let's not lose sight of this amazing discovery!" Nilah said.

Wick took a deep breath and relaxed. For the moment, it diffused the tension.

"So this is all an enormous diamond?" Wick asked. "The world's hardest substance?"

"More likely a mass of smaller diamonds," Nilah said.

"Still the world's hardest substance?" Wick asked.

"Yes, Wick, the world's hardest substance," she said.

In the silence, the awe of the diamond city returned, and the team fanned out to inspect the structures in hushed reverence.

Nilah ran her hands along the angled, glassy surface as she walked along. Maddix walked beside her. She tilted her head, listening.

"What?" Maddix asked.

"You hear that?" she asked. "Some sort of music. I didn't hear it before, but I hear it now."

Rohon, nearby, cocked his head. "I hear it, too."

Now everyone listened.

"It's a soft trilling," Bryer said. "Like stringed instruments . . . from space, I guess."

"If diamonds could sing, this is what it would sound like," Jovan said.

"Not singing," Wick said. "More like . . . a calling. Or something."

"Yes, our dear captain is right," Faber said. "There's a beseeching tone to the music."

Maddix watched as Nilah walked to the center of the temple courtyard. Rainbow beams rolled over her body and hair. The men watched her, stunned at the beautiful sight. She turned and saw them watching her.

"What is it?" she asked with a shy grin.

After noticing how the glittering light covered her, the men looked at the effect on their own bodies. They felt the collected warmth of the light.

Wick followed Nilah to the center. "These reflected beams are getting longer. The sunlight's almost gone. That low building over there will give us some shelter. Let's prepare for camp. We'll figure out our approach to this tomorrow . . ."

It was an odd sight to see people entering the diamond buildings. The cut of the diamond walls created a splintered view of each person. Not private, but not exposed either.

Nilah and Maddix cuddled up in a small room in the barracks. The glass surfaces were hard and uncomfortable, but it had been an exhausting journey, and they drifted off.

Maddix wasn't sure how long they had slept when something tore them awake. They jolted upright, ready for danger. But it was only Wick standing before them, smiling. In his hands he held out a spherical diamond the size of a cantaloupe.

"Where did you find that?" Maddix asked.

"Very funny," Wick said. "This is what the complex is made of. It's not a giant diamond carved into buildings, it's made of these. There must be millions of them."

Hundreds of cuts shaped the sphere as if the most expert jeweler had created it. In the moonlight, it gave off a special reflection. Its music was more intense.

Maddix stood. "So the city is made of big round diamonds?"

"Yep, whoever built this place used these beauties like bricks," Wick said.

"Where did you get that one?" Nilah asked.

"I wrenched it off the top of the city gate," he said.

Nilah and Maddix shared an uncertain look.

"Oh, don't get wobbly on me, you two," Wick said. "We don't need to tear down the entire complex. Just a few of these for each of us, and we'll be richer than any oil man or computer whiz. Hell, I could fill our cargo hold with these and it still wouldn't make a dent in this complex."

"True. I guess we're sitting on riches," Maddix said.

Wick handed the sphere to Nilah. She was uncertain at first, but holding the glittering ball, she couldn't help but gaze at it, mesmerized.

"I can hear its music," she said. "When I touch it, it's like I can *feel* its song."

Wick smiled.

"You can have the first one, Nilah," Wick said. "It looks good in your hands."

He smiled at them, nodded, and left.

Maddix sat with Nilah again, and they stared into the diamond sphere. Its beauty and the strange music that came from it hypnotized them.

Outside, the camp was active again as the men celebrated this alternative possibility. Nilah and Maddix came out to see what the crew was doing. Early morning light refracted through the trillions of diamond cuts in the complex. Wick and his men were busy removing diamond spheres from a nearby temple.

"You're not going to let them pull out all of those spheres are you?" Nilah asked Maddix.

"How can I stop them?" Maddix said. "Appeal to their sense of respect for lost cultures? If each man takes as many spheres as they can carry back to the ship, they will all be tied for the richest man in the world. There's no reasoning past that."

"And they're armed."

"Also very important to consider."

"What about you?" Nilah asked. "Are you taking any?"

He stared at the sphere in her hands. "Honestly, I guess I don't know. You?"

"Sounds crazy, but I'm more taken by its beauty than by how much money I could sell it for," she said. "If it took it, I'm not sure I could part with it for any price."

"Take one and sell one," Maddix said.

"Take one, sell one, donate a third," she said.

"Take one, sell one, donate ten," he said. "No one could criticize that. Right?"

"I guess not," she said.

Faber and Bryer joined them.

"Hello, doc," Maddix said. "Have you picked out some diamond balls?"

Faber chuckled. "Not just yet. I'm as excited as anyone, but I wanted to check with you first."

"I don't suppose we could prevail upon Wick to stop his men from tearing the structures apart until we've had a chance to make a survey?" Nilah asked.

"No, I don't think we would have any luck with that," Faber said.

"Didn't think so," Maddix said. "So what can we do for you?"

Faber and Bryer led the couple back inside the barracks. They sat in a circle.

"Now comes the part for which we pay you," Faber said. "What is this place? Any idea?"

Maddix and Nilah shared a look.

"No idea," Maddix said.

"It doesn't fit any known culture?" Faber asked.

"No. It's only resemblance to any known culture is the pyramid and temple complex," Nilah said. "But even at that, it's pretty generic."

"You call this generic?" Faber asked.

"The construction materials are off the chart, I'll give you that," Maddix said. "But there's no writing or inscriptions of any kind."

"No statuary or any indication as to who or what built it," Bryer said.

"It is a basic temple complex with no identifiable characteristics," Nilah said.

"Made of diamonds," Faber said.

"Made of lots and lots of diamonds," Maddix said.

"What about the music?" Faber asked. "It's coming from the diamonds, right?"

"I believe so," Nilah said.

"So creating music, that indicates communication, intelligence, does it not?" Faber asked. "I mean, we're way beyond the sounds of the wind through the trees. This is like whales singing. I get this feeling a conversation is happening."

"I'll agree, that's got me wondering," Maddix said. "It could be the wind. It could be vibrations through the diamonds that create the effect. We don't have the equipment to know for sure."

Faber sighed and thought about it. "This is the important question: You're sure there's no tribe or country that would lay claim to this?"

"We're not sure at all," Maddix said. "We're not even sure the island is uninhabited."

"How do we know the native population didn't run and hide when we came ashore?" Nilah asked.

"Or that they're ready to wipe us out for disrespecting their temple," Bryer said.

"We're really jumping the gun here," Nilah said. "We should take a sphere or two, take some photos and other samples and go home and see if we can track down any reference to this in the literature. I mean really dig deep and ask around to everyone we know."

Faber shook his head. "I'm afraid that can't be done."

Maddix stiffened. "Oh?"

"All I'm saying, Maddix, is that once word of this gets out, there will be a rush. Every country on earth—along with their military—will be in a race to get here. You think Wick and his men are being disrespect-ful? Ho-ho. Just wait. No, whatever we think is necessary to do, we must do here and now."

"Very well," Maddix said.

He rose and left the room. The others followed.

Maddix found Wick watching with a smile as his men stacked dia-mond spheres in piles.

"That's more than we can carry back," Maddix said.

"It will take more than one trip," Wick said. "But I want the cargo holds full."

"Letting your greed run away with you, are we?"

"It's not running away with me," Wick said. "I know exactly what I'm doing."

He gave Maddix a hard look. "The diamonds are coming back with us, Maddix."

"I had no plans to try to stop you," Maddix said. "All I ask is that you give us until tomorrow to study the complex before you take it apart. It may not mean much to you, but this is an important discovery for the world. We don't who built this place or why."

"I thought this was your area of expertise."

"Imagine how extraordinary it is when even we don't know."

Wick studied him for a second.

"All we want is one day," Maddix said.

Wick nodded. "Very well."

Wick called a halt to the diamond harvest. His men were suspicious, but Wick explained Maddix's position. They didn't show much interest in the advancement of knowledge, but they were tired. They shuffled off to the barracks for some sleep.

"Unknown history lying here for God knows how many years, only to be torn apart on the first day it's found," Nilah said.

"I sympathize," Wick said. "But once it was discovered, it was coming apart, by us or by someone else. Take heart, you are now among the wealthiest people who ever lived."

Nilah didn't seem excited by that idea. Wick watched, puzzled, as she returned to her room with Maddix. Bryer also left. Faber watched them leave. Before turning to return to his own room, he gave Wick a big smile and a thumbs-up. Wick felt relief. Faber was on his side, but he would have to keep an eye on his three scientists.

Jovan was missing when the expedition woke the next morning. At first, they assumed he had gone off to relieve himself or do some exploring. Maddix, Nilah, and Bryer began a proper exploration of the complex. They took pictures, conferred, drew maps, and jotted down copious notes. Wick sent Elroy and Parlan to look for Jovan when he didn't show up within the half-hour. Together, he and Rohon supervised the complex. Faber drifted around, asking questions and giving suggestions.

By mid-afternoon, the science team had finished their evaluation. Maddix and the others looked at each other.

"Anything else?" Maddix asked.

No one answered. They had done all they could think to do.

Wick joined their group. "Find anything interesting?"

Nilah shook her head, frustrated. "Nothing new."

"I wouldn't get too down in the dumps," Wick said. "If you had the ability to build something like this, it would serve as its own statement, wouldn't it? No need to sign your name to it. No ego. No glory. We're talking about minds on a different level here."

"That was our thought as well," Bryer said.

"You should join us," Maddix said.

Elroy and Parlan returned to the complex. Blood stained their pants and shirt. Their faces were grim and ashen.

"What happened? Where's Jovan?" Wick asked.

"Dead," Elroy said. "We brought back his body. It's outside the gates."

"What's left of it, anyway," Parlan said.

Wick absorbed the news. "How?"

"Looks like an animal got at him," Elroy said. "Or he got dipped in acid. Damn, it's a mess."

"So the island is not uninhabited," Maddix said.

"From now on, we stay in pairs," Wick said. "No one goes wandering out alone."

"How do we know he went wandering out?" Rohon asked. "How do we know something didn't come in here and get him?"

"Let's not get ourselves worked up," Wick said. "They're done examining the complex. Let's load up these spheres and pull out of here."

"It's better if we each take one and split," Rohon said. "That's plenty for our descendants to live on."

"The ship doesn't leave until I say so," Wick said. "And I want the cargo hold full. You want out of here? Load up fast."

As he spoke, Wick lowered his rifle until he could shoot anyone who rushed him.

"There's no need for that, Captain Wick," Faber said.

"I'm sure you'll all prove it to me, Doctor," Wick said.

For hours they lugged diamond spheres back to shore, where the boat took each load to the ship and returned for more.

On a return trip, Elroy and Parlan took a closer look around as they passed through the trees. The path from temple to shore was marked. They were tired and walked slowly.

"Check it out," Parlan said, pointing up.

A pair of pointed white stones curved downward from the bottom of one of the trees.

"What do you suppose that is?" Elroy asked.

"Looks like pearl or ivory," Parlan said. "Might be valuable. We could cut down a piece, show it to the experts."

"How you gonna get up there?"

"Should be easy enough to climb."

Parlan shimmied up the tree trunk until he could reach the ivory-colored protuberance.

"Looks like a giant bear claw!" he said.

He took a steady hold of the tree trunk with one hand and drew out his machete with the other. Elroy called out for him to be careful. Parlan examined the object.

"It has a hole at the bottom. A little one."

"Maybe it puts out that weird purple sap," Elroy said.

Parlan swung at the object. It cracked on the first blow. On the second, it came free and fell to the ground. Elroy stepped aside to avoid getting hit, then stood and stared at the thing. He didn't see the gush of jade-colored liquid that poured from the opening. Parlan called out for him to duck, but it was too late.

The green sludge hit Elroy. He screamed and flailed in panic and pain. Parlan watched in shock as the green stuff ate away at Elroy as if it were acid. Elroy fell to the ground dead as the acid ate him clean in half.

Parlan shook free of his terrified shock. He looked at the stop of the object as if it might attack him. Carefully, he came down the tree. By the time he reached the ground, Wick and Maddix had rushed to the scene and stood staring at Elroy's body in disbelief.

"What happened?" Wick asked.

Parlan explained what had happened. Maddix looked at the large curved, chunk Parlan had cut off the tree. He gazed up at the stump where one last green drop waited to fall.

"Step back, fellas," he said.

As they did, the drop fell and hissed when it hit Elroy's leg and burrowed into the flesh.

"Now we know what happened to Jovan," Wick said.

"Question is, was it an accident or deliberate?" Maddix asked.

"You're suggesting the trees attacked?" Wicked asked.

"This is venom," Maddix said. He pointed to the piece Parlan had cut free. "These cones are hollow in order to deliver the venom, just like snake fangs."

Parlan pointed up at the sharp white cones. "You're telling me those are fangs? Nonsense!"

"Captain, I suggest we get the hell off this island as soon as we can," Maddix said. "This was all too good to be true."

"No, we're finishing up the load first."

Maddix reached for his revolver. Wick lowered his rifle.

"If you kill me, Maddix, my men will kill you. We're talking about the greatest treasure in history. They'll do anything for it. You don't want to leave Nilah unprotected, do you?"

Maddix nodded. "True, your men would get me in a rush, but you'd still be dead. You want to spend your final moments thinking about the fortune you'll never spend?"

"So it's in each of our interests to get along," Wick said. "Very well. Let us do the heavy work, and you have my word we'll protect you and Nilah and the others. Then we'll leave."

"What about the tree venom?" Maddix asked.

"We'll just have to do our best to avoid getting under them," Wick said. "Do we have an agreement?"

Maddix holstered his weapon. It was decided.

After five more trips, they had loaded enough for each of them to have one hundred spheres. Maddix filled in Bryer, Faber, and Nilah on what had happened. They were unhappy, but agreed there was little to do but go along until they were back in the U.S.

Although the cargo holds weren't full, Wick called a halt to the effort. There was enough for each person to be richer than Solomon. Plenty to spread around to people in power and keep governments off their back. It was late afternoon.

Wick had provisions from the ship brought to the complex. He decided they would eat and then leave with one more load. Everyone ate and drank. Although somewhat subdued by the loss of Jovan and Elroy, Wick and his men chugged whiskey in celebration and in honor of their dead shipmates. Faber joined them for a toast or two, but kept himself dignified for the sake of his three scientists.

When Faber drifted away from the group, Wick followed him.

"Doctor Faber, I think it's time you told me about that map," he said.

Faber was startled. "I told you. I have a wealthy benefactor. It was he who came upon the map at a good price. The Spaniards drew it in the fifteenth century, based on a legend passed down on and on from Atlantis."

"Yes, you told me that. Now what is the real story?"

"That is the real story."

"I've lost two men today. Brothers. I've had a bit to drink, and I'm in a foul mood. I'm not as educated as all of you, but I know when someone isn't leveling with me. Call it instinct honed through a lifetime of dealing with dishonest people. Now tell me what you're not telling me."

Faber cleared his throat. "Is my safety guaranteed?"

"Not at the moment, but it can be if you level with me."

"I guess that will have to do," Faber said. "The map is not ancient, nor was it based upon legends from Atlantis or Lemuria."

"So it's a forgery?"

"Obviously it's a real map, Captain. We're here, aren't we?"

"Then why lie about its origin?"

"Because they created the map based on the ravings of a man possessed by a devil."

Faber waited to see how that was received. Wick thought about it and nodded.

"So this temple and what-not. It ain't exactly devoted to the risen Christ?" Wick asked.

Faber scoffed. "Hardly. You see, my benefactor's wealth has given him access to circles of knowledge and power that you and I can't even imagine. We're talking about a religion as old as the ancient flood. They give their own children to ancient gods from the world of spirits and even gods from other planets, other realities."

"So not only are we stealing from the gods, we're stealing from satanic gods?" Wick asked. "Nice of you to let us know the stakes beforehand."

"Oh, come now, Captain. This is not the treasure of a god who punishes for sins," Faber said. "This is the treasure of beings who steal human life, even those of their own children. If you can take the treasure and escape, it's all in fair play."

"I've seen men shake hands with the devil before, Doctor. Such bargains are always one-sided."

"So leave the spheres here," Faber said. "But allow me to take one or two of my own."

"We're leaving," Wick said. "Our fortunes will rise or fall together. But if you betray me . . ."

"I wouldn't dream of it," Faber said.

Wick returned to Rohon and Parlan to tell them it was time to go.

Maddix, Nilah, and Bryer sat and rested under a diamond overhang and watched the interactions.

"What do you suppose that's all about?" Nilah asked.

"Who knows?" Maddix said. "As long as we're leaving, I don't care."

"That's the plan, from the looks of it," Nilah said.

"I've decided I don't want any diamond spheres," Maddix said, out of earshot of the sailors. "Hell with it. I'd rather sleep at night."

"I don't want any, either," Nilah said. "But we should go through the motions of taking them, so Wick doesn't get suspicious. We can always donate them for study later."

"I might take one," Bryer said. "I have family that needs help. Real bad."

"Well, you should do what you think is right," Maddix said. "It's not for us to judge."

Bryer nodded and stood. He stretched and took a walk around the courtyard. Movement stirred behind him. Only Maddix saw it at first. A clattering sound got everyone's attention. They looked for the source and saw a spider the size of a moose tear into the clearing and attack Bryer.

The young man screamed in shock and pain as two fangs plunged into his shoulder and back. Wick and Maddix led the others in rushing to his aid. Maddix shot the monster, and it shuddered and released Bryer. Rohon and Nilah pulled him away from the attack.

The creature turned on Maddix, who shot it again until his pistol was empty. Wick pumped several rounds into the thing from his rifle. The other men joined fire.

By then, the creature wanted to escape. It fled back toward the pyramid, but after taking a few unsteady steps, it dropped dead to the diamond surface. Everyone was silent and still. They could hear only the soft song of the diamonds. It was more intense, emotional.

Maddix and Wick rushed to check on Bryer. The young man was dead. He was almost pure white. The puncture wounds were wide and raw. His chest and abdomen were sunk in, as if his insides had vanished.

"He was dead in seconds," Nilah said. "His suffering was great, but at least it was short."

Maddix returned to examine the dead creature. He looked back at Wick, who got the hint and joined him.

"Look at its fangs," Maddix said.

Wick looked close. Thick jade liquid oozed from the thing's teeth. Maroon sludge ran from the bullet wounds.

"Now look at its legs, its body," Maddix said. "The blood."

Wick put it together. "How could I have been so blind?"

"How long 'til nightfall?" Maddix asked.

"It's late afternoon. The sun's already going down."

The strange music of the diamonds rose in intensity as the wind picked up. The ground shook. Wick and Maddix turned to the others.

"Drop everything and run!" Wick said.

"There are white cones on the underside of the trees," Maddix said. "Don't run under them if you can help it."

"What's going on?" Faber asked.

"We're escaping judgment, Doctor," Wick said. "If you make it to the boat, I'll take you home. Until then you're on your own."

Parlan panicked and sprinted out of the complex without waiting for anyone else.

The rest of them ran out. Wick led the way. He shouldered his rifle. It would be no use against this newly discovered enemy. Speed was their only hope.

The tree trunks moved back and forth. A few rose out of the sand.

"What's going on?" Nilah shouted to Maddix.

"These things are alive!" Maddix said. "Don't get under those cones!"

"Why?"

"Because they're teeth."

A low, wet screech sounded from the treetops. Only now they knew it wasn't a forest they were trying to escape, but a swarm of giant, spider-like creatures.

Nilah's eyes grew wide at the realization. She didn't ask any more questions. She understood. So did the rest of the men.

Ahead of Nilah and Maddix, Wick keep up a fast pace. He dodged the creatures' legs and kept out from under the mighty fangs. The hideous teeth dripped venom in anticipation of a coming feast. The foul substance hit the sand and dissolved holes where it landed.

Maddix, looking up to avoid the deadly toxin, ran face first into a hairy leg and dropped to the ground. Nilah returned to help the dazed man to his feet. He rolled away just in time to avoid a hissing splash of venom.

Rohon and Parlan slowed their pace to escort Dr. Faber, but the old man was out of shape and fading fast.

"Hurry up, doc!" Rohon said. "I plan on getting back home to be a trillionaire! I ain't getting munched up here!"

Faber didn't answer. He had hardly any breath to speak. Parlan glanced back.

"Oh, no," he said.

Rohon looked back. A dozen smaller, juvenile creatures poured out of the temple complex and chased the men.

"Things just got worse!" Rohon said to those ahead. "Hurry!"

Faber looked back at the towering monsters as they closed in. He sensed Rohon and Parlan quickening their pace. Out of sheer panic, they would leave him behind. He had no wish to be next on the menu.

Parlan was closest to him. Faber kicked at Parlan's ankles, and he tumbled to the sand. Rohon looked back in shock as the creatures swarmed over the fallen Parlan. The young man's screams were mercifully short, and the monsters were distracted. Rohon cast a disbelieving look at Faber.

"Slowed 'em down, didn't I?" Faber said. "You want to live the life of a rich playboy, don't you? Well, you're welcome."

Rohon, looking up and ahead to dodge the hazards, drew out his pistol and moved out of reach of Faber.

"You touch me, Doc, and I'm tossing you to those things!"

Faber nodded. He was covered in sweat and gasping. Rohon shook his head.

"You're on your own," Rohon said.

He sped up and caught up to the others. Faber tried to call out to Rohon, but his breath was gone. A savage bolt of pain flashed through his arm and shoulder. He dropped to his knees. As he fell forward, his diamond spheres tumbled from his pack and fell to the sand. Faber fell to his face. The spheres lay just in front of his eyes. In his final moments, he saw a single ray of sunshine break through the mass of creatures and refract through the giant jewel. His face spread out in a weary smile as life faded. It was the last thing he saw. He was dead before he could feel the stab of numerous fangs into his flesh.

Rohon joined Nilah and Maddix. Wick was still ahead.

"Faber?" Nilah asked.

Rohon shook his head.

"It took us hours to get to the temple from the beach," Maddix said. "We won't make it."

Rohon and Nilah shared a look. They knew he was right. Ahead, Wick had moderated his pace as he ran between the towering legs.

"Something's changed," Maddix said.

They caught up to Wick. The captain saw that people were missing.

"Parlan? Faber?"

"Didn't make it," Maddix said.

"The further out we get, the less they're moving," Wick said.

The others looked around. He was right. The legs were still as before. The fangs were dry. Nothing dripped.

"A ripple effect," Maddix said.

"The creatures near the temple are active, but it's taking time for them to stir each other awake," Nilah said.

"The further away we get, the more deep asleep they are," Wick said.

"Does that give us enough time?" Nilah asked.

"No," Rohon said. "There are others. A group of smaller ones, like the ones that killed Bryer. Fast moving."

"Can we shoot them down?" Wick asked.

"Too many," Rohon said. "There has to be dozens."

"We're looking at another hour of running 'til we reach the shore," Maddix said. "And that's not accounting for fatigue."

Wick rested his hands on his knees. "There has to be another way or we're dead."

In the distance, they heard the approach of the younger creatures stampeding through the sand.

"Any ideas?" Nilah asked.

"For now, we run for it," Maddix said. "Maybe we'll think of something before it's too late."

The four of them sprinted toward the beach. The creatures came into view. They closed the distance with frightening speed.

Maddix looked back. "They're catching up!"

"Captain's falling behind!" Rohon said.

Wick, now the oldest of the group, panted and ran hard, but he lost ground. The creatures quickened their pace as though excited about catching more prey.

Rohon looked to Maddix. "We can't let him get chewed up by those things!"

"We can't fight them. That'd be suicide!"

Rohon stopped and aimed his pistol. "That's not what I mean."

He aimed to put Wick out of his misery just as Wick reached into his pack and started throwing diamond spheres at the pursuing monsters. When they were gone, he tossed the pack, then emptied his pockets of the spheres and threw those.

"No wonder he's running behind," Nilah said.

"Look!" Maddix said.

The brutes slowed their chase when the spheres fell before them. It gave Wick enough time to escape. He kept running and didn't slow down as he passed the others.

"Keep running, you idiots!" he said.

"You hear the music?" Nilah asked Maddix. "It's the music they're drawn to."

The creatures on the outer edges of the swarm tittered around, restless.

"See the ones on the outskirts of the group?" Maddix said. "They act like they don't know why the others have stopped."

"Maybe they have to be close to the sphere to hear it," Nilah said. "They're tied to the spheres."

The outer creatures came forward again.

"Let's think about it as we run," Maddix said.

Rohon was already off and away. He had caught up to Wick.

"Will they leave without us?" Nilah asked.

"Probably," Maddix said. "We'd better catch up."

Both were fit and did well running through the sand, although fatigue weighed them down. Maddix swung his pack around to his front while he ran. He pulled out a sphere and heaved it back toward the creatures. The first several of them stopped to regard the sphere. The others behind them flowed around and continued the chase.

"There's hope," Nilah said.

It took them thirty minutes to reach the shore. Shorter than they estimated, but enough to leave them sore, exhausted, cramped, and ready to pass out. By the time they broke the tree line, Nilah and Maddix had caught up to Wick and Rohon. The landing boat waited on the wet sand, ready to take them to safety. Three large canvas bags of diamond spheres sat within it.

Everyone knew the effect the spheres had on the terrifying inhabitants of the forbidden island. The four of them dashed to the boat. Wick unsheathed his knife and cut open one of the canvas bags. They tossed the heavy diamond balls as far as they could. The spidery monsters burst from the tree line and surrounded them.

Wick and the others carefully aimed their throws. They spaced the diamonds out to form a barrier. They emptied the bag. The monsters were captivated by the glittering globes sitting in the sand. For a few seconds, the four survivors caught their breath. Wick and Rohon pushed the boat into the ocean.

"Let's go," Wick said.

He fired up the motor as Nilah and Maddix hopped in. As the propellers churned and pushed the craft into the sea, the giant monsters along the beach stirred. The furry, oval bodies of the giants shook. Hidden eyelids lifted to reveal yellow orbs filled with anger. Unseen lips parted to show the horrible length of the fangs. A chorus of shrieks sounded out that so pierced the air that everyone had to cover their ears. The giants were so agitated they fought with each other and attacked their younger cousins on the beach.

Everyone looked back with sickened awe at the sight.

"Please tell me they can't swim," Nilah said.

"We're about to find out," Maddix said.

To their knowledge, none of the creatures entered the water to paddle along and chase after them. By nightfall, they were back aboard the *Karon*. After a light meal, Wick and Rohon took Nilah and Maddix to the cargo hold. The couple were nervous at what the sailors' intentions were, but when they saw the mountain of diamond spheres in the hold, they knew they were safe. This was the most valuable treasure ever found. Plenty to go around, and no reason to toss anyone overboard.

"Notice anything?" Wick asked.

Nilah and Maddix studied the gems.

"They look darker," Nilah said.

"Oh, yes I see," Maddix said. "I didn't notice at first under the dark light."

The diamonds were not as clear and bright, but had taken on a slight amber color.

"They lost a little whiteness as we left the island," Wick said. "They haven't darkened any more, so I think the effect is over."

"I can still hear the music," Maddix said. "Anyone else?"

Everyone could still hear it.

"Have the spheres lost their value?" Nilah asked.

"No, they're still giant diamonds," Wick said. "The ol' doc knew what he was talking about. I think they might be more beautiful like this. Either way, we're rich."

They watched Wick as he regarded his treasure hoard.

"Seems like you should be happier," Nilah said.

"We'll live well. For that I'm happy," Wick said. "And I can take care of the families of the men we lost. But it's the music that bothers me. What do you think it is?"

They thought about it.

"A form of communication," Maddix said.

"Between the creatures only? Or with someone else?" Rohon asked.

"Faber said someone channeling voices from another world dictated the map," Nilah said. "I thought it was just nonsense to keep from giving the genuine answer."

"The real answer is far more terrifying," Wick said.

Wick told them the demonic truth of the treasure map's origin.

"So we've taken more than giant gemstones," Rohon said. "We've taken things we cannot see."

"There's a conversation going on between those things and . . . what, I don't know," Maddix said. "Something bigger, badder, more dangerous."

"The diamonds were merely the means of transmission," Nilah said.

"So the second kind of music we heard . . ." Rohon began.

"Was made by those things," Maddix said.

"There are plenty of spheres left at the complex," Nilah said. "Their musical conversation can continue."

Wick nodded. "Yeah, maybe. But remember the precision of that complex. I wonder if we disrupted it."

"Maybe each sphere sings out and expects a response," Rohon said. "What if that response doesn't come? What might come looking for it?"

"Are you regretting your plunder, Wick?" Maddix asked.

"A little."

"Maybe you should dump it all overboard," Nilah said. "Let the ocean have them."

Wick shook his head. "No, I can't give up such riches, despite the danger. I'll live with the risk. Wherever I go, in my yacht or my castle on the mountaintop, I will always have a pistol nearby, along with my crucifix."

"You know bullets won't protect you," Maddix said.

"And what good is the crucifix to protect you against the sin of stealing?" Nilah asked.

"If all else fails, one bullet is all I need," Wick said. "I suggest you take the same precautions."

They cruised back to California. The song of the spheres continued without pause, haunting their thoughts and dreams, searching for an answer.

The Shudder

John was an old man near death, alone in his bed. His room was cozy. The nursing home was a timeworn castle. Stone and brick and wrought iron. Majestic silence. Repurposed for old timers near the end, like himself. Not quite a gilded cage, but pretty close. Better than a stale, antiseptic institution such as where his parents had finished their days. The ambiance of the place brought him his only enjoyment. He hadn't walked in months. Eating was a chore. Going to the bathroom was humiliation. The nurses had been by earlier to take him to the restroom. It was an exhausting ordeal, as usual. He hadn't been able to produce anything, which was more common than not. So they had returned him to his bed and tucked him in. His bladder would sound a phantom alarm in the middle of the night, and the whole futile, embarrassing routine would repeat.

As bad as the nights could get, afternoon was the most miserable time of day. John hated being so old and weak that he needed other people to attend to his basic needs. His usual routine after being returned to bed was to stew for a while about how much he hated his existence. He was worn out and isolated. It was time to go.

This day was different, though. Something in the air, or something that stirred in his body. Maybe it was his mind or his spirit. He wasn't sure. It didn't matter. Whatever the specific manifestation was, its cause was certain—he was close to the end.

Other residents, now departed, had told him of this feeling, how he could come to expect it one day. True, some people left with little warning. But sometimes, you just knew it was coming.

John nodded to himself, as if someone sitting next to him had spoken these sentiments to him out loud. He was eighty-nine years old. How many days was that? Who cares? What mattered was that this day was the last one. He was certain of it.

He glanced at the empty chairs in his room. They weren't the usual dull fabric and aluminum framed chairs. These were old and wood-carved, with nice velvet-covered cushions. They were also empty and cold. It had been a couple of months since someone other than a medical professional had been to his room. So much time had passed since a close friend or family member had been to see him that those visits dissolved into the fog of his old man's memory.

Julie and Michael were adults now. Had been for many years. When they moved onto their own lives, they had moved far from home. John liked to think it was just circumstance and opportunity that took them away. Part of him knew they felt no ties to keep them close. There had been no specific awful event or fight or betrayal. He had discovered, too late, that there was nothing mooring either of them to home. He had grandchildren that he'd met a time or two. They lived too far away for regular visits. He never had the relationship with them that he had with his own grandfather.

The empty chairs were too painful to contemplate, so he turned his gaze to the open window. It was winter. If the sun had been shining, that would've made it better. But it was gray, cloudy. So this is how it ends, he thought to himself. Alone and in crap weather. Not everyone dies in a blaze of glory. People like him just check out alone in their bed on a cold and cloudy day.

He fidgeted under his covers. He adjusted his blankets and tried to get comfortable. At his age, death had been looking over his shoulder for a while now. He didn't fear it. But there was a creeping dread that pounded at a door in his mind, a door he had shut and locked ever since he came here to finish out his life. So far he had kept that door shut, but he couldn't silence the patient, persistent knocking. No one called from behind the door. They didn't have to. It was memories that knocked at the mind's door. Memories that carried a reminder of The Imp.

John glanced at the open door to his room. He waited, wondering if the short little creature would come around the door post and stand there, staring at him with that hideous grin. The Imp had promised to return on John's last day. That had been ages ago, when John was only twelve. So long ago it didn't seem real. Memories from such a long-ago epoch couldn't be trusted, as a person's pain and desire altered the past to a more bearable form.

On this, though, John knew. The Imp had been real. What he gave to John was tangible and long-lasting. And his return visit was certain.

John looked away from the door. Let The Imp come if he will, John thought. I'm an old man. What will be will be. He also avoided looking out the window. Too depressing. He glanced to his side. The ceramic jar was still there, looking the same as when he'd first seen it, seventy-seven years ago. He didn't want to look at that anymore, but it was too late to give it away. The nurses never tried to take it away, because only John could see it.

Today, the last day of days, looking at the ceiling tiles would have to do. No, not even that. John closed his eyes. Already, tears trickled across his temple and tickled his ears.

He saw that day again. A few months past his twelfth birthday. It was summer. His chores done for the day, John sat at the end of the long dirt road to his family's farm. He worked on a broken bicycle chain. John was ready to put it back in place when he saw a strange person walking toward him. It came down the closest hill on the gravel road. It looked and walked like a child. It swung its arms in a wide arc, and it took bigger strides than its legs could accommodate.

John stood to watch the person approach. He thought it might be a child left behind by a school bus. Then he remembered it was summer. The buses weren't running. He'd known the neighboring families for years. This person wasn't one of them. He thought about running back to fetch his father. Old John winced at the decision his younger self made to face the creature alone. How things might have turned out differently.

It wasn't a child. It wasn't an adult, either. John thought it might be a little person. He had never seen one in person. John looked back at his house again. When he returned his gaze to the road, the little person had quickened his pace. It was a comical sight, but John didn't laugh. His parents had taught him better.

The little character was close enough for John to get a good look. He had reddish skin and wore an olive-colored, three-piece suit. A matching top hat fit snugly to his head. He smiled in a way John could tell was friendly, but carried an unmistakable aura of menace. Oh, if only he had run to his father right then.

Soon the little man stood before John. The almost-fixed bicycle lay between them. This was John's first and only meeting with The Imp. That's what John called him, for the odd creature never gave a name.

"Are you a man?" The Imp asked.

John frowned at that odd opening question and the low voice incongruous with the Imp's appearance. "No. Not yet."

"Has your father told you about being a man?"

"Some things. I guess. Yes."

"Has your mother told you about being a man?"

"Sure, a little."

"Then you're a man," The Imp said. "I can only talk to men. I can only see men. Therefore, you must be a man."

"Okay."

"A man decides things for himself. That's how it should be. Right?"

"I guess."

"I said, a man decides things for himself. That's how it should be. Right?"

"Right."

"Then I have something to offer you. You can take it, or you can say

149

no and don't take it. But it's up to you."

"I can't take anything without checking with my mom and dad."

"Then you're not a man," The Imp said. "I'll go somewhere else."

The Imp took a few steps to continue his journey, then paused. John was eager to know what The Imp offered. The Imp turned back.

"Of course, you've not been a man very long, have you?" The Imp said.

"No."

John wasn't sure when he became a man. He had recently turned twelve. Did that count as a man? He wasn't sure, but The Imp sure thought so.

"I'll give you another chance. You're not used to making your own decisions. I understand."

"If I take something, my mom and dad will want to know where I got it," John said.

"And you can't tell them about a funny-looking person like me?"

"Yeah. Sorry."

The Imp walked back and lifted to his tip-toes as if to share a secret.

"Well, what I'm offering you is a present for the mind. No one can see into your mind, right? That's all yours. No one can get in there whenever they like and ask where you got this or where you got that."

John considered that.

"Right?" The Imp asked.

"Right."

"I'll tell you what. You can look at it first. If you like it. You can have it."

John shrugged.

"I can tell that means a 'yes,'" The Imp said.

The Imp raised his hands and within them appeared a gray ceramic jar. It was the size of the middle kitchen canister, the one with sugar. Where The Imp had been keeping the jar, John didn't know. The little creature carried no pack or bag. His pockets weren't big enough. It appeared as if from thin air. John thought about asking where it came from, but was afraid of the answer. Another warning signal he ignored.

With one hand, The Imp offered the jar to John. With the other hand, he removed the lid.

"Just look inside," The Imp said.

"I can't take a jar into the house," John said. "My parents will wonder where I got it. You said this was something for my mind."

The Imp smiled, patient. "Just look."

John took a step forward and hesitated. "Nothing's gonna jump out, right?"

The Imp chuckled and shook his head. "I promise. It's safe."

John stepped closer, peered over the rim of the jar, and looked inside.

His breath quickened. His face went hot. Inside the jar was a swirl of color. Nothing extraordinary. Just the usual slate of colors seen everywhere. But the manner in which the colors arranged themselves were the most captivating John had ever seen or imagined.

"Beautiful colors, aren't they?" The Imp asked.

John nodded, transfixed. "I didn't think colors could be so beautiful."

A shudder took over John's body. His arms shook. He felt unsteady on his feet. His breathing hiccuped. The colors were so beautiful he wasn't sure he could stand it. Tears welled in his eyes. The colors were magical to him. The jar's palette had created a custom work of art to speak to his soul. Somehow, he knew that. As a farm boy, he loved the beauty of the landscape and nature, but this was on a different level. Did artists know colors like this? Was this the secret to beauty?

When the shudder passed, John felt dizzy and winded. The Imp replaced the cover and watched John for a few seconds.

"You like the colors, I see," The Imp said.

"Oh yeah. I've never seen anything like it. Those are actual colors?"

"Did you see any you've never seen?"

"No . . . just the same old colors, I guess."

"But put together in new and exciting ways."

"Yeah, I suppose."

"And the feeling they gave you? Did you like that, too?"

John felt embarrassed. "I guess I looked pretty dumb."

"Not at all. It's quite a feeling to see the colors for the first time."

John looked back at the house. He felt like he'd done something wrong, but couldn't figure out what that could be.

"So, you'll pour that color into my mind somehow?" John asked.

"Nothing like that," The Imp said. "If you want the jar, you can have it."

"But I told you, my parents will find it. I'm no good at hiding things. I don't want them to be mad at me."

"They won't be mad, because they'll never find it. It's visible only to you and me."

"It's magic?"

"Oh, yes."

"Why would you give me a magic jar for nothing?"

"It's my pleasure to do so."

"And nobody can see it? Not my mom and dad or sister or friends or anyone?"

"No one but you. In fact, once I give it to you, I'll be gone. For a while."

"For a while?"

"Oh, I'll be back."

"When?"

"On your last day."

"When I die?"

"Yes."

"What for?"

"To collect the jar."

"I'll have it until I die?"

"Most people keep their jars that long."

"Wow."

"Is that all right? It's part of the deal of having the jar."

John thought about it. "Okay, yeah. Sure. That seems fair. I won't need it anymore when I'm dead."

"No. You sure won't."

John looked around, trying to think of a reason to say no to the deal. He couldn't think of one.

"I'll take it!"

The Imp smiled. His teeth were bright white. "Excellent. Here, hold the jar while I do something."

The jar was light in John's hands, almost no weight at all. A two-foot long chain dropped from the jar and swung back and forth. John frowned.

"I didn't see the chain," he said.

"It's of no consequence," The Imp said.

In seconds, a manacle slapped around John's wrist. Fear gripped his body.

"Hold on. I didn't say you could chain me up!"

The Imp held up his hands. "Oh, it's not to worry! It's only for safety. You don't want to lose the jar, do you?"

"No, but—"

"And here's the key," The Imp said, placing a skeleton key in John's hands. "Take the manacle off anytime you like, and the jar will fade."

"Disappear?"

"Not completely. The jar will remain in view once you remove your manacle, but if you keep it off long enough, you might forget it. If you want the jar back, just return the manacle to your wrist, and all will be as it was. Most people want it back."

"Does anyone ever let it fade away and stay away?"

"Not many, but it has happened."

"People don't like the feeling the colors give them?"

"Strange, isn't it?"

John nodded as he looked at the jar.

"Whenever you want the shudder, just look into the jar. It's that simple. The colors will assemble in ways to give you that feeling. There's no end to what the colors can do. Remember that."

"I will."

John was eager to get the feeling again. He wanted it right away.

"So . . . are you accepting the jar?" The Imp asked. "Last chance!"

John took a deep breath and decided. "Yes. I want it."

The Imp was gone.

Through the rest of his youth, he constantly looked into the jar. As The Imp had promised, the colors repeated if that's what gave him the shudder. Or the colors would be brand new if he needed novelty. He fell behind in his studies. Not enough to fail, but it put him in the middle of the pack. He played the clarinet in the school band, but he stopped practicing and left music behind. He lost interest in sports. If he had free time, he wanted the shudder. The jar was always there. It required no work or payment. At least not with money.

Several times he realized the jar took too much away from him, that it wasn't free. At least once or twice a year he took the key and unlocked the manacle. The jar would fade and life improved. John took chances, made decisions, moved forward with life. But there was always a relapse. Stress would come, and he'd need the jar again, need to feel the shudder. He would look to his left, and there, as if it had never left, was the jar with the chain and manacle lying beside it. He returned the manacle, took his hit, and felt the calm sensation that made him forget life's troubles.

From that moment in the timeline of John's life, his aged mind could only remember things in pops and flashes. It was the usual stuff—finding love, losing it, finding it again. Friends came and went. New friends came and went. Friends and family died here and there along the way. He pushed ahead in life—getting a college degree and a job in an office, a wife and kids. He did the adult things, but in a rote manner. His marriage started as well as any but collapsed with great ferocity.

Through the motions he went. Looking back, John realized he never put his personal stamp on anything, never learned how good he could have been at music or sports, or, most painfully, how much richer his family life could have been. He thought things had changed for good when his kids entered his life, but after his divorce, they were in his life part-time and didn't appear to miss him much.

But the jar, and the shudder it gave him, took precedence over all. He gave great chunks of his life to the jar in time spent looking into it and enjoying the shudder.

Life was stressful. John had no delusions it was any harder for him than anyone else, but the jar was always there. The pleasure of the colors took away his stress, let off his steam. Sometimes, in an interesting development The Imp had never mentioned, the effect of looking into the jar wasn't the shudder, but a soporific, sedating effect, almost putting him to sleep or at least in a zombie-like, dazed state. How many harsh days and bad times had been eased by a peek inside? They were beyond counting.

The worst day of John's life was twenty years ago. He was sixty-nine, and one day he had spent morning until night staring into the jar. He didn't eat or drink. The house was dark when he looked up. The drapes were open, and the lights were out.

He blinked and made his way through the house, closing drapes and switching on lights and getting the house ready for nighttime. As he did, he noticed how quiet the house was. The kids' rooms were empty. They had moved out and away many years ago. His wife had been gone years before that and seemed thrilled with her second life and new husband.

Outside, it was cool. He studied the houses in the neighborhood where he had lived for thirty years. Every house had a new coat of paint but his. Kids had been born, grown, and moved on to their own lives. People had died. Neighbors had moved out and new neighbors taken their place, with a new group of young children. How had it happened so fast?

How did I become an old man without noticing?

The first thing that came to mind was the jar. It was his fault for leaning on it so much, but that was the source of his trouble. He glanced at his left hand, and the manacle became visible. He marched back into the house and freed himself, once again, from the jar.

Over the next several weeks he made phone calls and wrote letters. His ex-wife was polite and just as uninterested in being friends. His kids were happy to talk, but life was busy. They promised to call more often. They didn't. He got Christmas letters and the occasional letter from a grandkid. He stopped contacting everyone to see if they would keep up correspondence. If he didn't make contact first, no one took the initiative. The disappointment was severe, and he returned to the comfort of the jar and resigned himself to its company.

That had been twenty years ago. He could have great-grandchildren now for all he knew, and he didn't know. Presidents and bad news and good news and football champions and singers and movie stars and revolutions rose up and faded away. John told himself it was meaningless, mere hamsters on giant treadmills.

What did it matter now? Today was the last day. Nothing left to do but close one's eyes and shut the book and hope that he had done enough to enter a pleasant afterlife. And if by chance life was to be lived again, he would run from The Imp as soon as the thing came prancing down the gravel road.

The Imp.

He had outstanding business with the tiny creature. He had promised to return on John's last day and collect the jar. John couldn't dismiss that eventuality. The jar had worked as The Imp had promised. No reason to think John wouldn't see The Imp today. John planned to give the little man a piece of his mind along with the jar.

He took a long look outside. After a deep breath, he released the longest, saddest sigh of his life.

"Did you enjoy the jar?"

John swung his head to the doorway. There stood The Imp with that big, white smile, wearing the same olive suit and hat.

John glared at him. "You ruined my life. Take it and go."

The Imp unlocked the manacle and lifted the jar from the bed. He stood there for a moment, holding the jar and watching John.

"What?" John asked. "You've got the jar, now get out of here. If I weren't an old man, I'd throttle you."

"I'm sorry you feel that way," The Imp said. "But you need to come with me."

"I can't walk, you little ghoul."

The Imp took him by the hand and pulled. He had great strength for an Imp. It surprised John to find his legs help him upright. He hadn't been able to walk on his own for ten years.

"Come with me," The Imp said.

He led John through the door of his room. John frowned when they passed through to another, plain, room. They should be in the nursing home hallway.

"Where are we?" John asked.

"This is your new home."

"Huh? It's too late to move me to a new place. I'm too old."

"Oh, that? That was your old life. That's over."

John froze, absorbing the weight of The Imp's words. He knew it to be true.

"You mean, I'm—"

"Dead? Yes. I thought you knew."

"I knew it was coming, but this isn't what I expected."

"It never is. For anyone."

"You come for everyone?" John asked.

"Only those who gave their life to the jar."

John looked around the room. There were three plain walls, a floor with a simple chair, and a ceiling. The fourth wall was a glass window. Darkness lie beyond it.

"What happens now?" John asked. "Is this hell?"

"Watch what you could have become, John," The Imp said. "And you tell me."

Again, The Imp vanished.

Light came through the glass. On the other side of the window, a family party took place outside. John knew the setting. It was his backyard. The grass was greener and the hedges better maintained, but it was John's house. There was his wife, looking older but still beautiful and glowing with happiness. Michael and Julie were there, grown up and healthy. Their spouses were there. Little children of all ages ran about. A few were very little, and he assumed they were Michael and Julie's grandchildren. He had never met them, but somehow he knew who they were.

In the center was an old man. John looked at himself, the version of himself in this alternate reality. That older John was weary with age, but smiling. Kids and grandkids and great-grandkids took turns showering him with love. They crawled over his lap and squealed when he tickled them and gave them shiny coins.

John turned away from the scene and scanned the room. The Imp was not there. There were no doors on the walls.

He looked back to the family, his family. He wondered, were they real? Had he received access to a concurrent alternate timeline where he said no to The Imp?

John couldn't bear the thought of this being his eternity. Now that the jar was gone, he could turn his energy toward something else. Anything else. In desperation, he thought of options. Maybe he could leave this body. There had to be a way to reach out and leap out of this body, to join his mind to that of his counterpart beyond the glass. The jar was magic. Maybe he could find other kinds of magic. Was there a way? There had to be. He would find it.

He had plenty of time to think about it.

Tomb of the Black Cat

The black cat watched his family, the Carsten family, leave the house. He sat upright with his long tail curled around his paws as they bustled out the door. It was Halloween. They had a long night of fun ahead. He walked to the living room window after they shut the door behind them. He continued to watch them as they piled into the family car and drove off. Then he turned and walked away from the window. His name was Gideon. The Carstens were his family. They lived in Cinderbury, Massachusetts. Gideon had things to do.

Most of the citizens of Cinderbury were third generation and beyond. Many families traced their ancestry to the city founders who laid the first cornerstones after surviving the War of Independence. Newcomers were welcome. They just had to fit in. The ancient cobblestone streets, downtown brick buildings, and old Colonial homes had a way of knowing who belonged. When a visitor came over the old highway and saw the ancient town nestled in the New England hills, they knew they had entered another time.

It was a place that made an impression on you right away. If you came to town considering a new job, or you heard about its atmosphere and fall color, or needed a place to start over, you would love or hate it right away. The locals had observed this over the years. It wasn't anything they tried to influence. They shrugged it off as the city itself putting out a vibe to those it wanted and those it did not.

Local businesses offered all the goods and services the citizenry needed. Big-box stores were banned. They tried to make inroads into the local economy, but the aldermen always rejected them with a unanimous no.

Stately homes lined elegant boulevards. Ornate, wrought iron fences kept the dogs in. Gas-fueled street lamps kept everything illuminated at night. Emerald lawns were lush and well-maintained.

Cinderbury's residents were religious. Mostly Catholic and Orthodox, with a smattering of Protestant churches here and there. On every corner was a church, tavern, or a cozy, family-owned restaurant. They took seriously tradition and celebration. Everyone went all out for the holidays. The city had a warehouse full of decorations for the street lights and such.

But the two holidays that drew the most attention were Independence Day and Halloween. The first was obvious—patriots who had battled for and won freedom had founded the city. Halloween grew in popularity as the decades went by. In the current year, it was as popular as Independence Day. It wasn't hard to see why. With its old cemeteries and mansion-like houses, its craggy trees, ancient streets, and store fronts—not to mention its dazzling fall color—Cinderbury was a Halloween paradise.

There was a full week's worth of celebrations, parades, and activities leading to the big night. Nothing postponed Halloween. Not rain, nor snow, nor dark of night. On the big day, they held a town party and dance in the VFW hall. After that, everyone went home to either prepare to go trick-or-treating or receive trick-or-treaters. Teenagers continued to trick-or-treat even into their senior year. There was too much fun to let it go any sooner than you had to.

The Carsten twins, Lina and Aubrey, were fourteen and eager to trick-or-treat. The party was fun. It was always fun, with the punch and socializing and the live band. But what they really wanted was to join with their friends, sisters Josie, fifteen, and Penny, fourteen, and fill their treat bags. Later they would sort everything and trade candy. None of this could happen until the party was over.

James B. Christensen

Costumes for the Cinderbury Halloween were chosen with great care. Pre-fabricated costumes weren't banned, but they were frowned upon. Seamstresses made almost their entire years' earnings measuring citizens for costumes and sewing them. Enterprising high school students became proficient in make-up effects and earned a decent chunk of college money. Many had moved on to careers in Hollywood horror films.

Lina was an alien from a galaxy unknown. She had silver skin and purple hair. She walked planet Earth in a sapphire lamé gown, walking on purple platform boots. One of the aforementioned make-up artists had turned her skin silver with such skill it looked like real silver skin. A silver ray gun rested in a matching silver holster.

Aubrey was a werewolf ballerina. As was the custom, she eschewed a mask in favor of another high school buddy who turned her beautiful face into a canine monstrosity with top-of-the line fang inserts and fierce yellow contacts in her eyes. Crafting pointe shoes with werewolf claws bursting out took some doing, but the effect was convincing.

Josie spent most of her costume money on a colorful and exquisitely designed eagle costume. She wore a custom-made white feather cap. Her only reliance on make-up effects was a yellow beak, so skillfully attached to her face that you couldn't tell where the plastic met the skin. She walked on rubber eagle's feet that sprouted plastic talons.

Penny, to the consternation of her parents, commissioned a beautiful Cinderella costume, only to tear it here and there and splash it with stage blood. Cinderella's Revenge, she called it. If anyone cracked wise, she threatened to show them what happened to her stepmother and stepsisters. A large stage knife in her sash provided the exclamation point for her outfit.

At the party they danced together and waited for one of the boys to ask them to dance. While none of the girls got a specific invite, a gang of boys from their social circle showed up to dance with them as a group. That would have to count. Maybe at the Christmas formal the girls might get asked to a slow dance.

The townspeople had one bit of business to take care of at the city party before everyone dispersed. A group of town fathers took the stage. They were dressed unusually. Not Halloween costumes, as expected, but not everyday dress, either.

The four girls gathered near the front of the stage.

"You think one of us will see it this year?" Lina asked. "Cuz I wanna see it!"

"I want to make it my pet," Penny said.

"They've never found it," Josie said. "Because it isn't real."

"Oh, it's real," Aubrey said. "It's just waiting for the stars and moon to get right."

"Like tonight?" Lina asked.

"Don't know," Aubrey said. "I'll have to check."

A middle-aged couple walked by and admired their costumes. They grimaced when they saw Penny. She bared her teeth to show she'd applied fake blood there, too.

"Don't worry. It's fake blood," Josie told them.

"Is it?" Penny asked.

The couple moved on. The girls huddled together and giggled.

Six old people gathered on the stage. All aged sixty-five to eighty-seven. Three men and three women. All dressed as knights of an unknown realm. They wore black tin costume armor trimmed with silver. There were cloaked in capes, also of silver. They decorated the armor with symbols, created at random—no one would admit to knowing what they meant—and the armor plates were as thin as possible because of the age of those who wore it. A silver and black helm completed the ensemble. Besides those on stage, a dozen other knights dotted the crowd. They carried swords and unlit torches.

Mayor Losbert took the microphone and raised his hands for silence. He dressed as Paul Revere.

"Good evening, one and all, and thank you!" he said. "Welcome to another Cinderbury Halloween!"

The crowd cheered. The mayor again gestured for silence.

"I want to take a moment to thank everyone, once again, for you tireless efforts in making ours the best and oldest Halloween celebration in the country!"

Even the girls applauded that. They really were the best in the country.

"Soon it will be time for you youngsters to go forth and collect your goodies!" Losbert said. "For some of you it is your first year going door to door. For some, it may be your last before you age out. But let's work together to ensure it is the safest ever!

"But before we do, we will have our traditional Telling of the Tale, the story of how Cinderbury Halloween came to be. For that, I yield to the founder of our wonderful town, General Darius Davenport!"

Every applauded as Mr. Tarlup, a local actor, came onstage dressed in a Revolutionary War general's finest. He spoke in a deep baritone. Although everyone had heard the story many times, it riveted them.

"My fellow citizens. When I accepted General Clinton's surrender in 1783, we had still to face an enemy far more terrifying than even the most tenacious Redcoat brigade.

"A beast—thirsty for blood and hidden by the night, stalked not only my men but those of the British. It came by night and carried men away in their sleep by the light of the moon. This infernal enemy swore loyalty to no flag or king, but to its own appetites. Or so we thought."

Tarlup dramatically paced across the stage.

"The creature continued to attack even after arms were put away and they had laid the first stones of Cinderbury. In order to preserve peace for our descendants, I endeavored to learn the secrets of this beast and hunt it down. With the chief of the nearby Nipmuc tribe, I traveled along the Redmire River to the forbidden woods from where the creature came."

Tarlup glowered at the audience.

"The chief was privy to secrets carried down from his ancestors. With those secrets in hand, we could confront the monster and learn its true nature. It was a great black cat, as large as a grizzly bear."

"The Beast of Redmire!" someone shouted.

"Yes, the Beast of Redmire. As it turned out, the beast did not hunt for sport or hunger or protecting young, but to guard an ancient cave, a cave that bore so deep as to reach the fires of hell!"

People always twittered at the mention of hell. How dramatic.

"The beast guarded this cave and kept prisoner the hell hound that sought to escape. Our conflict brought us too close to the cave and threatened the beast's mission. And for that reason, men were killed so that evil could not escape.

"I will not tell you how we spoke to the beast. The Nipmuc chief swore me to secrecy. But we reached an agreement. We would aid the beast in its efforts to guard against the underworld and not interfere, even by accident. I pledged my own family name to that effort, and so I built the Davenport family mausoleum over the cave entrance, and the Redmire Cemetery grew around it. For these many years, the stone walls of my family vault and the sturdy fangs of the beast have kept the world safe.

"But as you know, Halloween night is when the veil separating the spirit world from the corporeal world fades to almost nothing. In our part of the world, this phenomenon lasts from midnight until six a.m. During that time, spirits of the dead rise from the ground and assume flesh and blood reality. They are aided by the spells and chants of living men and women of the occult who long for a world ruled by dark forces. Their mission is simple—kill the beast and let the hell hound escape.

Faced with that threat, we founded the Knights of Redmire."

Everyone cheered, and the Knights raised their swords. Swords, the girls noted, that were made of steel and whose edges were sharp.

"Every Halloween night, the Knights fight back against the invaders from the underworld and join with the beast to keep the hell portal blocked until the laws of the dimensional worlds reassert the normal order.

"For this reason, I must remind you the rules of Halloween night that have long been in place. All citizens—save for the Knights of Redmire—are to be off the street by midnight. The Knights have the authority to arrest and jail any stragglers. Power to the city will be shut down from midnight to six a.m. The street lamps will go dark during the same time period.

"I know in this day and age you have devices that record images. Don't bother. As I'm sure you know, these spectral beings that clash in the night do not appear in photos and videos as your friends and relatives do.

"So stay home and stay safe. The Knights will join with the Beast in fighting for good. We urge you to pray for their success. It is not uncommon to lose a knight in the course of our yearly battles. All across the country and the world tonight, witches and warlocks will pray to their gods. We must pray to our God, the one and only true God.

"And so my fellow citizens and Knights of Redmire, I bid you good night."

With a dramatic bow, Tarlup waved to the crowd and left to applause. Mayor Losbert returned to the microphone.

"It's that time, ladies and gentlemen!" he said. "Get out there and make it the best Halloween ever!"

Mr. and Mrs. Carsten drove the four girls home for a brief regroup before they went out.

The girls sat on the carpet and helped each other make last-minute hair and costume adjustments. As they took care of business they said hello to the small black cat who sashayed into the room. He had a tiny patch of white on his chest in the shape of a heart.

"Hi, Gideon!" Josie said.

Gideon crawled into Penny's lap and got comfortable. He had been a part of the girls' lives since they had memory. Mrs. Carsten had found him as a stray, wandering around their backyard. After searching without success for his rightful owner, Gideon became a part of the Carsten family. He was an adult when adopted by the family. The vet told them Gideon was the healthiest cat he had ever seen. They didn't how old he was.

While Mr. Carsten give the Standard Parent Lecture for Halloween Night, Gideon made the rounds from lap to lap. If someone didn't give him the attention he thought he was due, he pawed at their arm or face until they did. Of course, the girls always waited for him to do so.

There were lots of black cats in Cinderbury. There were no restrictions on adopting them, even at Halloween time. To mistreat a black cat would generate ill will among the townsfolk, to put it mildly. No one knew what might happen, because no one had ever mistreated one. Black cats had a special position in Cinderbury and acted like it.

The girls listened to Mr. Carsten. He was a Knight of Redmire and adjusted his armor as he spoke. He caught the sly smiles on their faces.

"I know you know what you need to know, and I know you know that I know you'll use common sense while you're out there," he said.

"Yes, father. I think," Aubrey said.

"If you need anything, I'll be patrolling Sawyer Street along the cemetery."

"Go along the usual streets," Mrs. Carsten said. "The neighbors will get a kick out of seeing you, especially if this ends up being the last year you want to go out."

"Can we go along the storefronts?" Lina asked.

"If you have time after walking the neighborhood? Sure," Mr. Carsten said. "But we want you home by midnight."

Midnight sounds late, but festivities ran late in Cinderbury. Besides, everyone was out until midnight, so things were safe.

"Do *not* go into the cemetery," Mr. Carsten said.

The girls agreed.

"Do *not* pass through the gates, even if the cool kids are doing it," Mrs. Carsten said.

The girls agreed again.

"Do *not* take it upon yourselves to solve any longstanding local mysteries," Mr. Carsten said.

"That's all the same thing, and we already agreed to it," Lina said.

"Okay, then," Mr. Carsten said. "Have fun."

The motley quartet bounded out of the house and down the boulevard. Mr. and Mrs. Carsten stood on the front porch with their arms around each other, smiling as they watched the girls knock on the first door. Soon the girls were out of sight. Mrs. Carsten turned to her husband and adjust a fastener on his shoulder plates.

"Go keep the beast safe and drive back the ghouls," she said, giving him a kiss.

"Will I win the affection of this beautiful maiden if I do?" he asked.

"You shall." She kissed him again, and her tone was serious. "Be careful."

He sheathed his sword and gave her a smile, and he left. She took a seat on the porch next to a bowl of candy and waited for little superheroes and monsters to arrive.

Lina, Aubrey, Josie, and Penny did well that night. Their sacks were full. They walked the same neighborhoods they always did. They were loaded with treats by then, but they went downtown to collect from the local business. Along the way, they stopped to chat with friends as they crossed paths.

They finished with fifteen minutes to spare before curfew. Their treat sacks were heavy. No one wanted to go home any sooner than necessary, but they were tired and they had been everywhere and seen everyone there was to see. They went back to the Carsten house.

"Time to go home, I guess," Aubrey said. "You guys can stay the night, right?"

"Yes!" Josie said. "Will your parents let us stay up as late as we want?"

"As long as we're quiet and don't watch anything we shouldn't."

When they got home, the porch light on the Carsten house was still lit. Everyone along their street was inside for the night. Mrs. Carsten wasn't around. She knew the girls would be back in time and didn't trouble herself to wait on the porch until curfew had passed.

They came up the front steps. After looking at each other to settle who would unlock the door, Lina took out her key and opened the door. A black shadow dashed through their legs and ran out into the night.

"Gideon!" Aubrey said.

The old black cat ran down the steps and along the street.

"We have to get him!" Josie said.

Lina checked her watch. "We only have ten minutes!"

"That's enough time," Aubrey said. "How far can he go?"

"Let's check with Mom," Lina said.

"Right," Aubrey said.

The girls crept into a dark house.

"Is Mom in bed already?" Aubrey asked.

"Maybe she's reading in bed or something," Lina said.

Penny ran off the deck and chased after Gideon. The other girls hissed at her to come back, not wanting to stir the settling neighbors. Penny did not slow down. Josie looked at Lina and Aubrey.

"I have to go after her!" she said.

Lina checked her watch again. "We have a few minutes. We can make it if we hurry!"

Lina and Aubrey ran after Josie, who ran after Penny. A cloudy mist had descended onto street level, and the four girls ran through the street like phantoms in the misty gaslight. Visibility was half a block, just enough to see where Penny ran.

She ducked away from the street toward a safety fence blocking a twenty-foot slope down toward the Redmire River. She was over the fence and running on the wooded embankment by the time the other three caught up. Again they called at her to come back.

"He ran towards the river!" Penny said, not letting up.

The other girls looked at each other, all of them hoping one of the other two would have the answer. Penny cried out in surprise.

"Penny!" Josie said. "Are you hurt?"

"I fell!"

There was no choice. They crawled over the fence and scrambled down the bank to find Penny. They found her halfway down.

"Watch out for the—" Penny said.

Lina, Aubrey, and Josie tumbled over a hidden drop-off and landed in a pile next to Penny.

"—drop-off," Penny finished.

"Thanks," Josie said. "Now we're stuck and we're dead meat!"

"Let's just climb back up and go home," Lina said. "I think we can still make it."

"What about Gideon?" Aubrey asked.

"He's lived on his own before," Lina said. "He'll find his way back. Look, if we don't get home before curfew, it's big trouble!"

"Uh, guys?" Josie said.

She pointed, and they looked. The drop off was too high for them to return the way they had come.

"Great," Aubrey said. "We'll have to find another way home."

"Any ideas, Penny?" Josie asked.

"No, I don't know my way through this part of town."

They listened to the whisper of the river as they tried to think of something. Lina threw her hands in the air and let them drop.

"The only way back up to a street is three blocks down," she said. "We're going to be late. No way around it now."

Penny stared at her "bloody" shoes. "I only wanted to help Gideon."

"It okay, but they might arrest us," Josie said. "You heard the mayor. The Knights can put us in jail."

"What about Dad?" Aubrey asked. "He's patrolling Sawyer Street, he said. He wouldn't arrest us, would he?"

"He might not have a choice," Lina said. "But I think he will just take us home."

"How far is it?" Josie asked.

"The river runs right down to it," Lina said. "Should take us fifteen minutes or so."

It was their only option. The riverbank was soft and treacherous, but the girls were careful and made their way to where the bank sloped up to Sawyer Street. There the path to the street was not as steep and they made it to the fence by pulling themselves along with tree branches.

They were ready to scale the fence when Aubrey gestured for stillness and quiet. She pointed to her ear. Listen.

"Going to be a bigger mess this year, Jon," said a voice.

"I know, Robert," said a second voice. The Carsten girls recognized it.

Dad? Lina mouthed. Aubrey nodded.

The girls got into position to see Mr. Carsten talking with Mr. Call, a second knight. Each had a sword in one hand and a torch in the other.

"The spiritual attack is more concentrated this year," Mr. Carsten said. "I'm worried it will overwhelm us."

"We'll know soon enough," Mr. Call said. "Only minutes or less until midnight."

The girls nodded at each other. It was time to come out of hiding. They climbed over the wrought-iron fence and fell to the sidewalk. Mr. Carsten and Mr. Call rounded upon them with swords raised. They frowned when they saw it was four teenage girls. Mr. Carsten's frown changed to shock when he recognized the girls.

"Lina? Aubrey?" he said. "And you two? What on earth are you doing out now? You know what time it is?"

"Gideon got out!" Lina said.

The knights exchanged a look. Lina explained their ordeal. Mr. Carsten waved her to silence.

"For crying out loud, girls. You know the trouble you're in?" he asked. "We have to arrest you and jail you. No family get-out-of-jail free cards."

"Go on, take 'em home, Jon," Mr. Call said. "No harm done."

"You'll be on your own," Mr. Carsten said.

"Just run 'em home and come right back. I'll be fine."

The street lamps faded and went dark as gas valves were shut in every neighborhood. Lights glowing in surrounding houses dimmed and went out as they cut the power. Moonbeams through the trees and filtered through fog gave off the only light.

"Too late," Mr. Carsten said.

"That's it, then," Mr. Call said.

The girls huddled close to Mr. Carsten. Mr. Call struck a match and lit his and Mr. Carsten's torches. Soon a ring of yellow light surrounded them in the mist.

"Now girls, this is dangerous business," Mr. Carsten said. "You stay behind me, no matter what."

The girls looked at each other.

"You're not really fighting anything, are you?" Aubrey asked.

"I thought all that talk of ghouls was just a bunch of bullstuff," Penny said.

The knights shared a look. Mr. Carsten shook his head with a weary smile.

"We're in a war of dark and light forces, Penny," he said. "And the outcome is never guaranteed."

A strange sound got their attention. The sound of movement. Something on the street. Not footsteps, but lazier, more draggy. Shuffling.

"They're coming," Mr. Carsten said.

"You should take the girls into the cemetery," Mr. Call said. "To the tomb. At least you'll be near the beast if he comes."

"What?" Aubrey asked. "That's the last place we should go!"

"It's the safest place when every place is dangerous, my dear."

"He's right, Aubrey," Mr. Carsten said. "You girls come with me."

Mr. Carsten led them up the street. He held the torch at arm's length in front of him. A shambling, rotting humanoid wearing a dilapidated suit staggered out of the mist. The girls screamed. Mr. Carsten swung his sword and beheaded the creature. He handed the torch to Lina. Then he removed the thing's legs at the knee.

"Come on!" he said, taking back the torch. "And stay out of its reach!"

They continued to the cemetery.

"Robert!" Mr. Carsten called over his shoulder. "Everyone! It's started!"

He led them to the top of a paved ramp to the cemetery gates. They went through. Tombs and gravestones sat along the fog-shrouded ground that swept back out of sight. Several torches broke the gloom, and the girls knew other knights were present.

"So the ghouls are real? Far out!" Penny said.

"They're real and they're far out, all right," Mr. Carsten said. "And they're deadly. We—meaning myself—have to remove their arms and legs so they can't attack."

"How do you kill them if they're undead?" Lina asked.

Mr. Carsten swept the torch in front of him. They crept along to avoid any ghouls waiting to leap from the shadows. Ahead, a massive mausoleum came into the light. Everyone knew that was the tomb of Darius Davenport and his family.

"We don't kill them," Mr. Carsten said. "We disable them and let them lie on the ground until the witching hours are over."

"Six a.m.?" Josie asked. "Six hours?"

"I'll get you home sooner if I can," Mr. Carsten said.

They came to the mausoleum and stood on a small paved courtyard at its entrance. He shuttled them into the courtyard with their backs to the portico.

"Stay here and behind me," he said.

They nodded their agreement. He turned his back to them and scanned the graveyard. Other torches glowed in the distance. Some close. Some far. They swept back and forth, waiting for the ghouls to descend on the cemetery.

The girls looked at each other.

"What's worse," Josie asked Mr. Carsten. "The waiting or the fighting?"

"The waiting."

A wind gusted through the cemetery trees, taking the misty fog with it. The moonlight, along with the combined torch light, gave everyone a full view of the cemetery and Sawyer Street below. The girls gasped at the sight.

Several dozen lumbering ghouls shuffled toward the cemetery. There might have been hundreds.

"Remember, girls, stay behind me," Mr. Carsten said.

"Is this what happens every Halloween night?" Penny asked.

"Yes," he said.

A ghoul appeared in front of Mr. Carsten. He dismembered it with his sword. Another materialized after it. That one was also cut to pieces.

The girls huddled as the battle began. Other knights shouted a war cry as they engaged the attacking ghouls. The creatures had one goal— to get to the Davenport mausoleum so they could free the hell hound trapped below.

Mr. Carsten held his position, determined to keep the girls behind him safe, so he held his position and let the ghouls come to him. Robert Call jogged through the cemetery, cutting and slashing as he went, and joined the battle at Mr. Carsten's side.

"Thought you could use a hand," he said.

"I appreciate it," Mr. Carsten said. "Lots of beasties this year."

"A decisive move being made by our witchy friends."

The two knights, along with others spread out around the cemetery and city streets, battled against the ghouls. They kept coming. It was a relentless assault. The ghouls cared nothing for their own well-being. They weren't alive. They were slaves, disembodied spirits with a temporary body willing to sacrifice for the forces of evil.

The girls watched the fight, both frightened and fascinated. This was a side of the world they had read about in tall tales, but never seen nor suspected to be real.

A wave of ghouls came through the front gate, chasing a group of knights in front of them.

"There might be too many this time, old friend," Mr. Call said.

"Speaking of old friends," Mr. Carsten said. "Where is our old friend?"

As if to answer, a long, low growl cut through the chaos. For a moment, everyone—even the ghouls—froze in place.

"He's here," Mr. Call said.

The girls almost laughed at his dramatic tone.

Heavy footsteps crunched through the leaves. They were not the steps of a bipedal being, but something that walked on four legs.

"Is it the beast?" Aubrey asked.

On their right, a giant shadow blocked out the moonlight as it passed. It was sleek and black. It paused at the mausoleum and looked at the girls. They shrank back under the gaze of the brilliant yellow eyes. It bared its fangs in a roar and continued on.

"I'm thinking that's the beast," Lina said.

The beast crouched and readied to pounce.

"Stay out of the way!" Mr. Carsten said.

The beast jumped into the air and landed on a hapless ghoul. The giant cat tore the ghoul to pieces and moved on to the next one.

"There's still too many," Mr. Carsten said.

The knights backed into a group near the mausoleum. They formed a defensive circle and kept fighting. The beast continued to make quick work of the invading ghouls. Despite the effective defense, the ghouls just kept coming, wave after wave. Soon, they broke through the knight's circle. The girls watched, horrified, as knights fell wounded in the battle.

The ghouls poured through the defenses. The situation was desperate, and Mr. Carsten worried the girls were in grave danger.

"Run!" Mr. Carsten said. "Run home if you can!"

By now, he figured the ghouls wanted only to free the hound. He swung his sword back and forth in blind hope that he'd cut the invaders down. His energy ebbed. Six a.m. was far away. The knights would never last. He shuddered to think of a world where the hound was loose.

The girls saw no way out of the cemetery. Fear did not allow their legs to move. Together, they backed into the corner of the courtyard, clung to each other, and awaited their fate.

Out of the shadows and chaos of the battle, the beast bounded toward them and stopped. It tore apart several ghouls and relieved Mr. Carsten. The girls stared, transfixed, at the large black cat as it watched them with large, almond-shaped yellow eyes that glowed.

The cat let out a long feline scream at the girls. They ducked away from the horrible power of it.

"I thought it was on our side!" Aubrey said.

After the scream, the cat sprinted away and tackled another ghoul.

"I feel weird," Lina said.

"Me, too," Penny said.

The girls agreed that everyone felt weird.

"Uh, Josie?" Penny said. "What's happened?"

Lina and Aubrey looked at Josie in shock. A second before, Josie wore an eagle costume. After the beast's scream, she *became* an eagle. The girls sized each other up. Each had become a living version of their costume.

"Dad?" Lina said.

Her skin was no longer painted silver. It was silver. Aubrey—now a real werewolf ballerina—tried to call for her dad, but her voice could only produce a canine roar. Mr. Carsten turned around. His eyes went wide.

"What's happened?" Penny asked.

Her face had assumed a dark, murderous look. She held up her knife. It was now steel instead of plastic.

"It's the power of the beast," Mr. Carsten said. "Use it against them, not me, yeah?"

The girls looked at each other and grinned. Lina raised her ray gun and fired at a ghoul. To their delight, a red beam shot out of the gun with a trill and blasted off a ghoul's leg.

"Let's get 'em!" Josie said.

Penny had already left the group. She attacked a ghoul and cut off its legs.

Josie took to the air. If a knight was in danger, she would swoop down, take a ghoul or two in her large talons and carry them away. Then she dropped them on the wrought iron spikes, impaling them so they couldn't hurt anyone.

The knights watched in shock as the girls aided the fight. Judging by their reaction, this was something new. Aubrey roared as she leaped fifteen feet or more to take down a ghoul. She tore them to pieces with her claws and jaws. Lina stalked among the gravestones, shooting off limbs and not missing once. Penny only had her knife, but her super-power was gusto. With their help, the tide of battle turned.

Mr. Carsten and Mr. Call exchanged a smile as if to acknowledge that they just might make it through the night victorious.

Under the branches of a willow tree next to the Davenport tomb, the air spun as fog rose from the ground, forming a mini-tornado between the branches and the ground.

"What out, Jon!" Mr. Call shouted.

Out of the fog came a procession of ghouls. They came straight toward the tomb.

"More invaders," Mr. Carsten said. "The powers of darkness have bet everything on tonight."

He readied his sword, but there were far too many monsters. Other knights came running, but they wouldn't get there in time to save him.

Aubrey roared at Josie and pointed at her father. Josie got the hint and coasted down. She grabbed Mr. Carsten by the shoulders and whisked him to a safe place next to Mr. Call.

Lina fired at the ghouls as the other girls attacked too. A second wave of ghouls swarmed the giant cat. They were torn to pieces, but the goal was to keep the cat busy.

The ghouls reached the portico of the tomb and broke the locks.

"They're going to get in!" Mr. Call said.

"We have to stop them," Mr. Carsten said.

"There's too many. We can't."

"We have to try."

Mr. Call followed as Mr. Carsten ran into the mass of ghouls. They were easy to defeat, but the men were outnumbered. The creatures were at a near-frenzy anticipating the release of the hound. They pulled the door open and poured into the mausoleum. In the center of the floor was a large tomb. It was that of Darius Davenport. Three ghouls pushed the tomb aside and revealed a hole with an earthen staircase descending into the ground. Action and chaos ceased as a chilling howl filled the night air.

"The hound," Mr. Call said.

"We're too late this time, old friend," Mr. Carsten. "We have failed."

The girls renewed their attack. The ghouls, having accomplished their goal of opening the tomb, grew lethargic and were easy to cut down. They merely stood and waited for the hound to rise from the depths of the tomb.

"What now?" Mr. Call asked. "Can we fight the hound?"

"It's a creature of the abyss," Mr. Carsten said. "It would take an angel."

"Should we run?"

"Could you live with yourself if you did?"

The men took a deep breath. Other knights joined them. Everyone was weary, but mindful of their duty. They looked at each other. For generations they and their ancestors had fought this Halloween night battle and done well. Now they faced the prospect of fighting the battle for the last time and losing. The hell hound was here to wreak havoc upon the waking world. They readied their swords and prepared to face the hound.

As if to mock them, the hound howled again. The sound shook the walls of the tomb. In the hush that followed, everyone heard the clicking of claws as the hound pawed its way up the ancient steps.

But this time, a terrible feline scream answered the howl. Even the ghouls parted the way as the mighty black cat padded toward the tomb with menacing grace.

The hound appeared in the portico. It was the size of a horse. Its fur was rust-colored. The eyes glowed red. It bared its horrible long fangs. They dripped with strings of saliva.

The Beast of Redmire crouched, its ears flattened, its great tail waggling, ready to spring. The hound barked with the power of a dinosaur's roar.

The beast sprang at the hound. Everyone backed away, astonished at the sight of such a titanic battle. Feline claws tore into the hound. Both creatures sank their jaws into their opponent's flesh. The roars of the furious beasts tore at their ears.

Lina's ray gun sounded as she fired at the hound. The girls and the knights turned to look at her.

"Well?" Lina said. "Let's help!"

With the ghouls in a lethargic state, it was easy to finish them off. It took time, but as the spectral animals brawled at the tomb's portico, they finished the job. Soon, there was nothing left to do but watch and hope the beast gained the advantage.

"The hound's trying to escape," Mr. Carsten said. "You notice that?"

"And the beast keeps cutting off its path," Mr. Call said. "If it chases the hound back into the tomb, should we close them both in?"

The girls protested.

"I don't think we have a choice," Mr. Carsten said.

Mr. Call nodded. They watched for their opportunity.

"They're both hurt," Josie said. "How is that possible?"

"When they assume flesh, they assume blood as well, I suppose," Mr. Carsten said.

The beast saw an opening and lunged at the hound's throat. The canine roared and gurgled in primal fear and rage. The beast pushed the hound into the tomb with is muscular back legs. The hound's paws scrambled and slipped on the dirt steps as the beast shoved it back toward a yawning hole.

"Shut the door!" Mr. Call said.

"Wait!" Mr. Carsten said. "Look!"

The beast released the hound at the edge of the hole. The hound stood on the steps and caught its breath. For a few seconds, the animals stared at each other. Both were wounded and bleeding. Suddenly, the beast screamed. The hound backed down a few steps. It barked, but the sound was not as fearsome as before. It knew it had lost. The beast advanced and screamed again. The hound retreated further.

The knights entered the tomb behind the beast. One more terrible scream from the beast and the hound had retreated out of sight. The knights rushed in a pushed the tomb back in place.

No one was sure what the beast would do next. The evening had been one of broken precedents. It turned and left the tomb, stopping before the girls. They smiled as the creature looked each of them in the eye. There was something calming about its gaze. First Aubrey, then the rest of them, brushed their hands along its fur. Just like Gideon, the beast raised its back into their petting, as if he welcomed it. Then it walked past them, speeding into a run. It paused to look back at them and growl, then jumped the high wrought iron fence and ran into the night.

The knights came out of the tomb and closed the portico door.

"Dad?" Lina said. "The ghouls. They're gone."

Everyone looked around. The cemetery was empty of any evidence of the battle except for a few wounded knights. No one had died this time.

"I thought they could be in our world until 6 o'clock," Josie said.

"The battle has been won," Mr. Call said. "The veil between worlds is closed. I guess that made the difference."

Mr. Carsten put his arms around his daughters. "Let's go home."

Everyone was achy and tired as they entered the Carsten house. It had been an incredible night, but there was still Halloween work to do. The girls dumped their candy on the carpet and discussed what movie they wanted to watch. Each one made the case for a movie related to their costume. They watched one for each. Mr. Carsten observed them with a smile.

"Don't be too loud, girls," he said. "I need sleep."

He left the room and went upstairs to bed.

"It's going to be hard to see your dad as just a patent attorney from now on," Josie said.

"I know, right?" Aubrey said.

The opening credits ran on the werewolf film they chose. As they watched, they sorted out candy they wanted to trade.

"We never found Gideon," Lina said.

"I hope he's okay," Penny said.

"He's tough," Josie said.

"Yeah, he hid in a tree during that ruckus at the cemetery," Aubrey said. "He'll be back by morning."

They munched candy and watched the movie at low volume. The flickering black-and-white images made them drowsy. Josie and Penny were asleep before the end of the first act.

It was quiet in the house then, the kind of quiet that still crackles with energy after a day of excitement. It was now November and when Cinderbury was awake for the day, it would be time to focus on other holidays. Lina and Aubrey stretched and yawned in their living room campsite. Their energy ebbed and their eyelids grew heavy as the movie marathon outlasted them. Together they joined Josie and Penny in dreamland among a pile of pillows, blankets, and trusty stuffed animals.

A series of creaks sounded from the hallway. The sisters stirred back to partial awareness.

"You hear that?" Lina whispered.

Another creak. The floorboards. Slow, but heavy footsteps.

"Someone's coming down the hall," Aubrey said.

"Dad?" Lina called out.

No answer. The girls turned to watch the darkened hallway, half-frightened of who or what might come through. It was Halloween, after all.

Another couple of loud creaks, and all was quiet again. The girls looked at each other, puzzled. Gideon rounded the edge of the sofa and meowed. The girls smiled, delighted at his appearance. He crawled into the middle of their little campsite and soaked in the attention.

While petting Gideon, Lina looked back at the hallway.

"What?" Aubrey asked.

"Something big was in the hallway," Lina said.

Aubrey thought about it.

"But something small came out," she said, looking at Gideon.

The old black cat turned in three circles and curled up on the blanket between the girls. The girls continued to pet him as they watched TV. They were awake again.

"Oh no!" Aubrey said.

"What is it?"

"Gideon has an owie! Look! A bunch of them!"

"Poor thing!" Lina said.

Gideon had scratches and bite marks. The wounds were raw. There was no bleeding. Gideon had cleaned himself. The girls looked at each other, confused. Then realization dawned on both of them at once.

"Oh my God!" Aubrey said.

"You don't think . . ." Lina asked.

They looked at Gideon.

"Hey, boy, have you been out getting in fights with monsters?" Lina asked.

Gideon meowed. It was an answer only he understood.

Aubrey stroked his back. He leaned into it and purred.

"Good boy."

Gideon lowered his head to sleep. Soon the girls followed. The five of them slept through the night. In a moment they always remembered, they were warm, safe, and together.

About the Author

James B. Christensen is a novelist, screenwriter, musician, husband, and father of twin daughters. He is the author of *Honeymoon Phase*, a supernatural romantic comedy; *The Vessel*, an occult horror thriller; and *October Nights* and *October Nights 2*, the first two installments in the ongoing anthology series. He lives in Omaha, Nebraska.

Visit *jamesbchristensen.com* to sign up for his monthly newsletter and stay informed of upcoming releases. When you sign up, you'll receive a free copy of the novella, *The Sky Critters of Brockton County,* exclusive to subscribers.